CW00495538

# MISCHIEF AND MISTLETOE

*Forever Yours Series*

## STACY REID

**MISCHIEF AND MISTLETOE** is a work of fiction. Names, characters, places, and incidents are the product of the author's imagination or are used fictitiously. Any resemblance to actual events, locales, or persons, living or dead, is coincidental.

Copyright © 2019 by Stacy Reid. All rights reserved, including the right to reproduce, distribute, or transmit in any form or by any means.

Edited by AuthorsDesigns
Copy Edited by Gina Fiserova
Proofread by Monique Daoust and AW Consulting
Book cover designed by AuthorsDesigns

*Dusean, always and forever.*

## FREE OFFER

### SIGN UP TO MY NEWSLETTER TO CLAIM YOUR FREE BOOK!

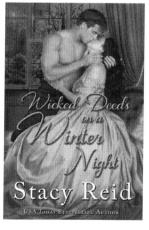

To claim your FREE copy of Wicked Deeds on a Winter Night, a delightful and sensual romp to indulge in your reading addiction, please click here.

Once you've signed up, you'll be among the first to hear about my new releases, read excerpts you won't find anywhere else, and patriciate in subscriber's only giveaways and contest. I send out on dits once a month and on super special occasion I might send twice, and please know you can unsubscribe whenever we no longer zing.

Happy reading!
Stacy Reid

PRAISE FOR NOVELS OF
STACY REID

"**Duchess by Day, Mistress by Night** is a sensual romance with explosive chemistry between this hero and heroine!"—*Fresh Fiction Review*

"From the first page, Stacy Reid will captivate you! Smart, sensual, and stunning, you will not want to miss **Duchess by Day, Mistress by Night**!"—*USA Today bestselling author Christi Caldwell*

"I would recommend **The Duke's Shotgun Wedding** to anyone who enjoys passionate, fast-paced historical romance."—*Night Owl Reviews*

"**Accidentally Compromising the Duke**—Ms. Reid's story of loss, love, laughter and healing is all that I look for when reading romance and deserving of a 5-star review."—*Isha C., Hopeless Romantic*

"**Wicked in His Arms**—Once again Stacy Reid has left me spellbound by her beautifully spun story of romance between two wildly different people."—*Meghan L., LadywithaQuill.com*

"**Wicked in His Arms**—I truly adored this story and while it's very hard to quantify, this book has the hallmarks of the great historical romance novels I have read!"—*KiltsandSwords.com*

"One for the ladies...**Sins of a Duke** is nothing short of a romance lover's blessing!"—*WTF Are You Reading*

"**THE ROYAL CONQUEST** is raw, gritty and powerful, and yet, quite unexpectedly, it is also charming and endearing."—*The Romance Reviews*

OTHER BOOKS BY STACY

The Earl in my Bed

*Wedded by Scandal Series*
Accidentally Compromising the Duke
Wicked in His Arms
How to Marry a Marquess

*Scandalous House of Calydon Series*
The Duke's Shotgun Wedding
The Irresistible Miss Peppiwell
Sins of a Duke
The Royal Conquest

*The Amagarians*
Eternal Darkness
Eternal Flames
Eternal Damnation
Eternal Phoenyx

*Single Titles*
Letters to Emily
Wicked Deeds on a Winter Night
The Scandalous Diary of Lily Layton

CHAPTER 1

*Two weeks before Christmas.*

It was a scandalous and audacious plan, which could be fully attributed to last week's dream, and Miss Callisto Middleton, known as Callie, was quite determined for it to bear fruit. Her mother deserved happiness and with an earl too! Impossible, some would say, but her papa had always impressed upon Callie that her tenacity in the face of adversity was her most admirable quality. And it was that quality, along with her winsome smile, golden-brown eyes, and good-natured charm he had believed would see gentlemen falling over themselves to offer for her at her debut years ago.

Of course, it hadn't gone as dear Papa had planned. But her failed Seasons and unmarried state were not Callie's current concern. No, that went to her mother, Viscountess Danby, the unhappiest

1

woman in the countryside. And Callie knew exactly what her mama needed—a beau to call her own.

A hitch found its way in Callie's heart, and she brushed it aside, having already accepted that it was altogether fine for her mother to remarry only five years after her father had gone on to his rewards. The directions of her current ambitions came from Papa, and whenever she dreamed of him, good tidings always followed.

Only two years ago, she'd dreamed of Papa directing her and Mama to Gloucestershire. Callie had insisted they visited the area where they'd found the most charming and affordable ten-room cottage to be their home. Then six months ago, another dream where she saw her papa floating on clouds at a particular section of the woody forest surrounding their homes. The next day Callie had visited and saved a child from drowning in the river.

Surely the dream of her papa standing from a cliff and smiling down at her mama who had been laughing in the arms of the Earl of Deerwood, their neighbor, *was* providence. Callie had realized her mother's tendre for the man a few months now. Why, whenever Mama saw him, the viscountess would blush, and even upon a few occasions, had stammered in her replies. Her mama, blushing as if she were a debutante and not a mature woman of two and forty years!

But it was more than that...the earl made her mother laugh, reducing the shadows of grief and melancholy which had lived with her since losing her husband, and replaced it with something sweet, hopeful, and tender. She was still an exquisite woman, beautiful, and elegant. With her pale blonde hair and glistening green eyes, she looked many years younger than her actual age. Callie was convinced she deserved another chance at happiness in a loving marriage. Then the earl had invited them as a family to a house party in his home, and after much anxious indecision from their mother, they had arrived yesterday and had settled in nicely. There were at least thirty guests, including the earl's son and his daughter.

"I must get them together," she said, nibbling on a piece of lemon cake.

"Get who together?" Letitia demanded, popping a tart in her mouth and crunching.

Callie scowled at her sister, who, despite stuffing her face with confectionary, looked so pretty. "You should try to eat in a more ladylike manner. All of Mama's efforts at teaching you proper etiquette are being wasted."

Letty rolled her eyes and tossed her ebony curls. "We are alone, Callie."

"Still—"

Letty waved her hand in a frustrated gesture. "There is no still about it! You are trying to distract me. Who must you get together?"

Callie glanced around the tastefully furnished private parlor, knowing very well they were alone, but a lady could not be too careful. It was also one of the few rooms not decorated with holly and mistletoe. "I aim to play matchmaker."

Letty gasped, a glint of mischief appearing in her light brown eyes. "Good heavens! With someone here at Lord Deerwood's house party? How fun that would be. Nothing amusing ever happens to us! Playing matchmaker is vastly more entertaining than strolling about the damp lawns and playing parlor games."

"Yes, it is someone here," Callie said, laughing at her sister's exuberance.

"You are far braver than I credited you for," Letty said with an approving nod. "Is it Vinnette you are helping along? She is so painfully enamored with Viscount Sherbrooke! I was heading to the library for a book late last night, and I saw her sneaking into his room, and she was only in her night rail!"

Callie gasped, lowering the fork with a piece of cake on it to her plate. "Why, I never! Are you certain, Letty?" Another of their neighbors, Vinnette, was the daughter of Squire Brampton, the second-largest landowner in the area. They had become wonderful friends in the two years Callie's family had settled in the area.

An image of the shockingly handsome viscount floated in her thoughts—midnight black hair, magnificent blue eyes, sharp cheekbones, and an arrogant yet sensually curved mouth. Her stomach did a frightening little flip. The heat of a blush rose in her cheeks, and she fought to suppress her reaction.

It had bothered Callie very much that she found Lord Deerwood's son so appealing.

"Did...did the viscount allow her inside?" she queried tentatively, wondering at his intentions. The viscount did not live at his father's estate, but his visits were frequent. Vinnette had not told Callie they had an attachment. *Oh, Vinnette, what are you thinking?*

Her sister nodded, a pink blush staining her cheeks. "I was awfully shocked at such a wanton display of improper behavior. But she is our friend, and we must help them to the altar considering what we must assume had happened in his room last night."

Callie cleared her throat. "Well, we know the purpose of a well-intended house party is to indulge in wickedness!"

Letty wrinkled her nose. "I am not entirely certain Mama would have brought us here if *that* were common knowledge. Nor do I think that is his lordship's intentions."

That was an astute observation, but Callie had pleaded with her mother to attend the earl's annual Christmas house party after receiving the invitation. Perhaps her mother's reluctance had been rooted in all the possible scandals on attending a house party! Though Lord Deerwood's December parties had no salacious rumors attached to them to her knowledge. It was a tradition which his countess had started, but he had continued even though she had gone onto her rewards a little over ten years ago. It seemed the earl and his family had gotten the news of her passing on Christmas Eve while the family had awaited the doctor's report.

For the last few years, the earl and his daughter had hosted a lavish house party which lasted for two weeks leading up to a Christmas day feast, which surely rivaled the table of the Queen Victoria. Despite the coldness of the season and the occasional falling snow, the earl's guests would spend their two weeks of holidays hunting, riding, and even playing indoor games. In the evening, formal dinners would take place followed by music, some impromptu dancing, charades, whist, and games of billiards for the men where they could smoke indoors without fear of censure.

Many whispers suggested the earl held the house party to distract himself from the painful memories surrounding the yuletide season. For those invited, who did not care to spend Christmas alone or with intolerable family or wanted to be there for the earl, made their way to his palatial country home for the festivities. "It is not Vinnette I wish to help snag her beau. Though I will certainly speak with her to find out what it is that she wants."

Letty paused in taking a sip of her tea, holding the cup in midair inches away from her lips. "Not Vinnette?"

"No."

Letty frowned, wariness settling on her lovely

face. "Then, who? We barely know anyone here, and I am still in disbelief that they invited us. The earl is well known, and only those in good standing are welcome. I cannot credit anyone from Society should recall us to their minds, though I am pleased we got asked to come this year."

"It is Mama," Callie whispered, clasping her fingers tightly over her teacup.

Letty stiffened, lowering the tart to her plate and brushing the crumbs from mouth. "*Our* mama?"

"Yes," Callie replied, meeting her sister's startled gaze. "I suspect she is in love with Lord Deerwood."

Letty appeared dazed. "There is a rumor that he is an arrogant sort of man, very haughty and concerned with rules and propriety."

"We didn't see any evidence of such a disposition when he welcomed us yesterday." The earl had almost appeared nervous, and his eyes had strayed to her rosy-cheeked mother often in the few minutes he'd made introductions to his other guests. At dinner, he had paid particular attention to their mother, who had seemed a trifle flustered with his attentions.

"Well, we hardly know him!"

"Exactly, Letty," Callie replied with a wave of her hand. "We absolutely cannot believe in any gossip about the earl. We could, however, trust in Mama's judgment. It is wholly unlikely she would admire anyone so haughty and prideful as the rumor suggests."

Letty sighed. "He is also a man in his prime and is

considered a most eligible *parti*. He is only seven and forty and still so handsome and dashing. Why would he ever consider our mother? You go too far with your ambitions, Callie!"

She stood and made her way over to the floor-to-ceiling windows overlooking a section of the palatial estate. The light snow they had received this year had already started to thaw, and despite the chill in the air, the earl's guests were enjoying the outdoors.

A group of well-wrapped guests played croquet on a lawn swept free of snow, and others practiced archery in good humor, laughing at each other's hits and misses. Even in the distance, she saw a few people rowing on the lake which had not frozen this year. Merriment danced in the air. Despite being several days away, Christmas—its feel and scent—surrounded the earl's country home. Holly, garlands of ivy, pinecones, and sprigs of mistletoe attached with bright-colored satin bows seemed to decorate every room. Fresh-cut red and white roses which must have been grown in glasshouses to bloom at this time of year had been artfully arranged, and in the evenings, the gardens and surrounding parklands were festooned with hundreds of decorative lanterns and candlelight, which cast an ethereal glow on the remaining patches of snow and the reflecting lake.

"'Tis the season to be hopeful," she said, staring at their mother, who sat under a gazebo near the pruned rose gardens, a book in her hand. The earl in question strolled with a lady along the edge of the lake, and at times her mother risked glancing at them. It was painful and almost embarrassing to watch her mother's evident tendre for the earl.

Lord Deerwood, in turn, seemed aloof as he strolled with the animated Miss Penelope Barrows. That lady was eight and twenty, and Callie had heard her only yesterday state her determination to marry by next year. It seemed Miss Barrows had decided on catching the earl. It was hard for Callie to determine if his affections were engaged. He seemed to be politely listening, but was careful not to stroll too close beside Miss Barrows. In truth, his manner suggested an indifferent listener.

"Mama has little to recommend her to become the wife of such a man," Letty put forth, coming to stand beside Callie. "I cannot credit you would be so bold as to even contemplate it."

"Mama is the daughter of a baron and was the wife of a viscount. Even if we are not wealthy, we have respectable connections!"

Letty worried at her bottom lip with her teeth. "Still, Lord Deerwood is—"

"Oh!" An unidentified emotion squeezed at Callie's heart. "Look at the earl, Letty!"

Her sister leaned forward, and commented with wonderment in her voice, "He...he is staring at Mama when he thinks no one is observing. Oh, Callie, I daresay he likes Mama too!"

The expression on the earl's face was one of acute longing. Unfamiliar emotions twisted through Callie, and she pressed a hand against the cool glass of the windows. A few light snowflakes danced in the air before settling on the thick verdant grass where a large peacock, with its iridescent tail spread preening, lingered.

"I daresay he admires Mama most ardently," Callie stated, an unexpected hunger crawling through her veins. Many days she too had wondered what it would be like to be courted, to be sent flowers, to be taken on lengthy walks in the park, to be on a bench with her beau reading whilst he listened with rapt and sincere attention. She was four and twenty and had never experienced such delights. What would it be like to dance the waltz, and to be kissed? She closed her eyes, pushing aside those dreams which seemed so unattainable, given the family's dire circumstances for the past five years.

Their mother lowered her book, and when she looked toward the earl, he hurriedly glanced away. Letty giggled infectiously, and Callie smiled.

"How silly they are being," her sister cried. "What are we to do about it?"

"They only need a little nudge!"

"How are we to do *that*?"

"Perhaps with a few well-placed notes and twigs of mistletoe."

They shared a glance, and then dissolved into laughter.

"Oh, Callie, this is recklessness on our part. And surely too improper and wicked of us."

Miss Barrows chose that moment to slip and cry out. The earl attended to her with urgency, and soon afterward swung Miss Barrows into his arms and marched toward the main entrance.

"That lying wretch," Letty cried. "There is nothing wrong with her ankle. She has pretended to be hurt to be in the earl's arms."

"Do you believe me now that Mama needs our help?" Callie said, a lump forming in her throat at the expression of loss and mortification on her mother's face. "Will you be my helper?"

Letty took a steadying breath. She had always been the more modest of the two sisters, much more like their mother in her temperament and appearance. Gentle and kind, and demure, especially in the presence of others. Whereas Callie had always been *frightfully improper and too much like your papa*,' which was a common refrain of their mother's.

"Yes!" Letty said.

With her sister behind her, Callie hurried from the private parlor and rushed down the long hallway, grateful they did not encounter any other guests. The scent of lemon wax and pinecones was redolent on the air, and in the distance, someone played a lively tune on the pianoforte in the music room.

"I will write a note, one to Mama and the other to the earl. See that they are delivered with the utmost discretion, Letty!"

"I will ensure it," her sister promised.

Callie ran up the stairs and made her way to the

chamber she shared with Letty. Once there, she sat before the small escritoire, withdrew a sheaf of paper from the drawer, and dipped the quill in the inkwell.

*Dear Lord Deerwood,*

*I've long admired a man of your amiable, good-natured, and passionate qualities. I've often imagined we might stroll by the lake and indulge in artful conversations about our mutual likes and dislikes. While games of charades, whist, and music in the drawing-room promise lively fun, perhaps we might meet in the conservatory after dinner this evening? I will await you at half-past nine. I do hope to see you there, my lord.*

*A lady of sincere affections.*

CHAPTER 2

G raham George Wynter, Viscount Sherbrooke, stared at his father, the Earl of Deerwood, in mute amazement. The man appeared decidedly flushed, and from how he repeatedly raked his fingers through his black hair and patted his top jacket pocket, he was utterly agitated. Graham stretched his legs and leaned more against the cushion of his chair.

"Does your note bear unpleasant news?" he asked, taking a careful sip of his brandy.

Graham had been at a newly purchased country estate in Hampshire, which its former owners sold due to bankruptcy. He had been working alongside the architects on the renovations, when he had opened a rambling letter from his father, one that had been bloody difficult for him to decipher. Certain phrases had caught at his mind and had filled him with alarm. And he was not a man prone to an excessive display of emotions.

*"I've met the most wonderful woman."*

*"I think it might be time I marry again, except I cannot tell if she is indifferent to me or interested."*

*"I've asked Alice to plan a house party for Christmas, and I mean to invite Lady Danby and her charming daughters."*

*"I've taken the liberty to procure a special license, but I do not believe she might have me."*

Those were the phrases that had stuck with him as he rode in the ghastly weather as fast as the road conditions allowed for several days while overnighting at inns. Perhaps the most alarming bit in his father's hasty letter was this plan to marry a lady who seemed indifferent to his affections. His father was a man who fell easily in love. Graham scowled, recalling the last fiasco and the scandal it had wrought.

Within a few weeks of meeting one Lady Wilma Prescott—a celebrated beauty in the *ton*—his father had declared himself besotted and had offered for the lady. She was twenty years his junior and had happily accepted. Then she had the temerity to slip beneath the sheets of Graham's bed, all with the plan that they would have a rousing affair while she was married to his father.

He'd kicked her from his room with the threat he would ruin her should she try to further entrap his father. She had tearfully apologized, but Graham had been immune to her pleas for his forgiveness and silence. Because at four and twenty at the time, he had endured over the years many women trying to marry his father for his title and wealth. But that lady had been the boldest and most scandalous one. Graham had informed his father of his fiancée's duplicity, and his father had withdrawn into himself, but at least he had forced Lady Wilma to officially end the engagement. That had been two-and-a-half years ago, and his father's letter had been the first since then to mention he had a recent love interest.

"Father," he said in a carefully composed voice. "You are out of sorts."

The earl folded the letter, placed it in his top pocket, and turned to face him. "I did not expect you to travel down because of the weather. I know you have little patience for house parties and the sort."

"We've always spent Christmas together."

His father, still a handsome man in his prime, smiled. "We do, my boy, but I still thought you would have sent down some excuse to not attend."

Graham took another sip of his brandy. "Your letter warranted me making the trip."

His father cast him a probing, considering glance. "You are familiar with our neighbor, Lady Danby, and her two daughters?"

A vague image floated through his thoughts, then a pair of bright brown eyes and a dimpled smile came into sharp focus. Ah yes...he'd met a Miss Callie Middleton several months' earlier. She had been walking through the woods, which abutted their estate. Though she had been in a simple white day dress adorned with a yellow ribbon, her prettiness had stuck him. He'd watched for several minutes, charmed by the animation of her features as she'd read her book. Her face had expressed a unique reaction with each page she'd turned—a furrow of brows, irritation perhaps, then that biting of her bottom lip as if nervous, then that wide smile. At one point, she had gasped, screamed a bit, and pressed the book to her chest, and the happiest of sighs had escaped her. That oddity had amused and charmed Graham.

The young lady had looked up then, and her eyes had ensnared him with their expressive beauty. She had dipped into a curtsy; unaware he had watched her for near thirty minutes. He'd tipped his hat in a polite gesture and walked away. When he'd glanced back, she had stood there, staring at him, her face one of surprised contemplation. He'd seen her a few times since then in the village, but he had made no effort of introducing himself.

"Are you referring to the widowed viscountess?"

A flush worked itself over his father's cheekbones, and he glanced into the fire. "A most... pleasant, and amiable woman, if I've ever met one. And kind with such considerate manners. And so beautiful."

That bit resonated with such reverence, Graham sat straighter in the high wingback chair. "I see. And it is her you are wondering if you should...make your new countess?"

His father sighed. "I suppose you think I am a fool over love."

Graham winced. The very words he had roared at his father a few years ago when the earl had planned to offer for another woman, Lady Fairclough. Graham had struggled to understand how his father had considered marrying at least three different women in the last ten years. It seemed a bit inconstant to Graham. With each new lady love, the earl informed his children of his intentions, making them a full part of his decision-making. With each failed arrangement, his father had kept searching, and it seemed his entire concentration was on getting married.

It had baffled Graham, for his father already had his heir and a beloved daughter. What use was marriage to the earl at this stage? Then he'd realized his father was lonely and wanted more than just the comfort of a mistress to warm his bed. The shock of that awareness had left Graham restless for weeks, and he had tried to spend more time with his father and ignored the pursuit of frivolities in Town. He'd been at his father's side for the last several months learning estate management and helping him with his motions for the opening of Parliament. He'd recently taken over most of the duties of the earldom, leaving his father to live a more leisurely life and to be assured that when Graham inherited, all would be well.

But he had still sensed his father's dissatisfaction

with life. "I do not think you are a fool father...you are simply searching for something." *Something that I want you to find.*

A singularly attractive smile crossed the earl's face. "And I believe I have found it."

"You have?"

His father's features softened even more. "Yes! She is *wonderful*, and I am certain she is the one for me."

Graham grimaced. "So you have said...at least twice before."

His father flinched, and regret burned in Graham's gut. Surging to his feet, he stepped toward him. "Father, that was tactless—"

His father held up a hand, cutting off his words. "No. This time..." the earl took a deep breath. "This time...it is like how it was with your mother. Maybe even deeper."

Guilt and something unfathomable darkened his father's blue eyes. Graham relaxed his fingers, which had tightened around his glass. Never had his father compared the women he'd courted to the great love he'd had for Graham's mother. He was unsure how to feel about it. "I see."

His father cleared his throat. "I would like you and Emma to spend time with Amelia...Lady Danby."

Spend time with the viscountess? His father had never requested such a thing before. It flummoxed Graham for several moments. "Is our approval necessary, father?"

A sight frown creased the earl's face. "No, but I would still like to hear my children's valued opinions. If...if it works out, she will also be a part of your life and Emma's."

Graham nodded, some of the tension easing from his shoulders. "And the note?"

His father hesitated before plucking it from his pocket and handing it to Graham. He scanned the letter asking for a clandestine meeting. An elegant flowing script scrawled the words, but it was not signed. Whoever it was, wanted his father to meet them in the conservatory in less than an hour. That hint of deception had anger curling through his gut. Why did it not similarly annoy his father?

*Who are you?*

"We are at a house party. I hardly think such subterfuge necessary," he scoffed, rather irritated with the author. "Surely you must suspect their reason for wanting such a meeting."

The earl seemed contemplative. "Someone...a skilled *waif*, slipped this note in my pocket! How alarmed and intrigued I was to find it. Except I...I am uncertain the author of this note is who I am dearly hoping it is!"

"The viscountess," Graham said. "You are hoping it is from Lady Danby."

"Yes," his father snapped on an aggrieved sigh. "I do...I hope it is from her! For it would tell me clearly she has some feelings for me that are beyond friendship and neighborly courtesy."

"Is she the sort to send such letters?" Though the wording was innocent enough, it could be a trap by anyone of the marriage-minded ladies in attendance. Twice now, his father had almost gotten caught by a woman of dubious standards and with only greed in their hearts.

His father tugged at his cravat looking distinctly befuddled. "She *is* shy but comes alive within minutes of conversation. Then I see no shyness, only her good-natured charm, and vivacity for living...and blushes," he relayed this with a bit of wonder and a smile on his lips. "Lady Danby blushes so prettily if I stare at her too long, or if I pay her the sincerest of compliments which she deserves. I am uncertain she would be this bold."

Yet hope lingered in his voice that the lady had indeed decided to be daring.

"Why not ask the viscountess how she feels?" Graham suggested. "She is not a debutante who needs to be protected from such advances. She is a woman of sense and mature years; such a question will hardly send her running."

A tic jerked in his father's cheek. "I tried," he said with a gruff voice. "She loved her husband very much. Only...she has only lost him these past five years. Whenever we speak, the viscountess always find a reason to slip him into our discourse. I admire how much she loved him, but it almost makes me believe she might not be willing or open to the idea of me courting her."

Graham recalled the rumors which had surrounded the viscountess's move to Gloucestershire. She was without funds, her widowed portion only enough to maintain the appearance of bare gentility. Her older daughter had her come out some years ago, which had not netted her any new connections or a match, and the younger girl had never had a Season in London. Now there was little opportunity for the viscountess to secure respectable matches for them.

The lady must be desperate for marriage into a well-connected family. Either the viscountess or her daughters would do for an earl. He glanced down at the invitation to a tryst in the conservatory once more. How far would the widowed viscountess be willing to go?

"If you wish to see for yourself, Father, go, but be mindful of the lady's intentions."

His father sighed. "I will be. Once I see that it is not Amelia...I will politely extricate myself from the situation and hope no one is around to witness what they might perceive as misconduct!"

And without a doubt, the identity of the author would be revealed, and Graham would know who to keep a close watch on, for this person would most likely be prone to more mischief for the remainder of the house party. Was his father walking into a compromising situation that might prove difficult to extricate himself from?

*I'll be damned if I ever allow that to happen*!

# CHAPTER 3

Almost thirty minutes after speaking with his father, Graham stood in the conservatory, positioned behind some large fir trees which had been cut to be decorated and placed in the drawing-room, music room, and the entrance to Holliwell Manor. Ever since they had spent Christmas in Germany with one of their uncles, his father had adopted the tradition of decorating such trees in the yuletide season. It had made his mother, who was German, thrilled, and as a family, they had continued the tradition after she had gone on to her rewards. Graham was closer to the door which opened into the garden, and from his discreet vantage point, he observed the lady who had entered moments ago.

His heart jolted, and a heavy unexpected disappointment lodged in his gut. It was Miss Callie Middleton still garbed in the bright pink dress she had worn to dinner, her hair piled in a riot of becoming curls, with several wisps dancing about her face. She was petite, the top of her head would probably brush his chin. Her skin was pale, her lips lush and sweetly curved, her figure, though slender, had more than a handful in all the right places. The lady held a basket in her hand. She rested it on a table revealing fresh-cut roses from the hothouse and a pruning shear. She rifled through the contents of the basket, and he arched a brow when she withdrew several sprigs of mistletoe.

*Good God*. Her intention was apparent. How many ladies had he dodged since his arrival who attempted to use those damnable mistletoe berries to request a kiss or be bold to take one? Even last night, the squire's daughter had knocked on his door, and he had tugged her into the room after hearing footsteps in the hallway. Miss Vinnette Brampton was the sister of his close friend Thomas. Graham had been amused and appalled in equal measure at her surprising brazenness. But the girl had been suffering from a case of jealousy and heartbreak when the man she loved shifted his attention to another. After drinking several glasses of pilfered sherry and armed with a fistful of mistletoe, Miss Vinnette had planned to soothe her wounded pride with kisses from him!

Even now, the memory of her silliness had a sigh of exasperation escaping from Graham. It was befuddling how everyone seemed to accept that piece of twig was an excuse to throw caution and propriety to the wind. He wasn't the sort to seduce his friends' sisters, so after lending a listening ear for several minutes, he'd ensured she reached her room undiscovered.

A sharp grunt snapped his attention to Miss Middleton. She was dragging a wrought-iron chair from near the grate to the door. She hopped onto the chair and then took it a step further by balancing on the chair's armrest. It rocked precariously, and she muttered a word no lady should know before making a soft triumphant sound. She mounted the leaves and berries above the door, and with a wide grin, jumped from the chair. Graham marveled she had not slipped. She looked up at her work and did a happy little twirl.

He felt mesmerized. Perhaps it was the sense of happiness and expectation in the air. She dragged the chair from out of the way, then strolled to the windows with a frown on her pretty face. The lady reached into the deep pockets of her dress and fished out a pocket watch. She leaned forward, almost pressing her nose against the glass. Unexpectedly she lurched upright and to his amazement clapped her hands in unmistakable glee. She rushed toward the exit that would lead her to the side gardens. The lock refused to budge, and her expression of excitement eased to annoyance. After childishly kicking the door, she hurried in his direction.

Graham stepped behind one of the fir trees. It barely hid him, and he expected her to see him right away. Instead, when she was almost on top of him, she turned and peeked around the tree. It seemed the lady, too, was hiding. His curiosity mounted. An entrance to the conservatory opened and closed with a quiet snick. Miss Middleton held her breath, impatiently tapping her feet.

"Finally," she muttered with a content sigh when another person entered the glasshouse.

He resisted the urge to look at the newcomer, directing his complete regard on Miss Middleton.

"Lord Deerwood...I mean...Robert...I...I hoped it was you," a very, breathless voice gasped.

There was a rustle of movement.

"Amelia, my dear, how happy I am to see you," his father said warmly and with heavy relief in his tone. "I almost did not come and then decided to at the very last minute."

Ah...so the lady was the viscountess. The man should be happy, indeed.

"I got your note—"

"I got your note—"

They faltered, and the viscountess released a shaky laugh. Graham dared to step closer to Miss Middleton so he could see above her head. Lady Danby and his father stood under the arched entrance, facing and gazing at each other. How... utterly besotted they appeared.

"You got my note?" the viscountess squeaked.

"Yes," his father said with a frown. "Did you not send me this?"

He plucked the note from his pocket and handed

it to her. The viscountess laughed. "*I* got a similar note."

"Ah...so someone is playing cupid," his father said, reaching out and tucking a tendril of the viscountess's hair behind her ear. "Are you very disappointed I am not the author of such pretty words?"

Even from where Graham stood, he could see the flush of pleasure on the lady. She clasped her hands before her, and her teeth worried at her bottom lip. How young she appeared, certainly not the look of a woman who had two grown daughters. She was flushed, her eyes bright, her countenance one of nervous expectation.

"I am glad this person sent us notes," she said, with a small smile. "Whoever it is. They had the courage to do what I was thinking."

His father reached out and took one of her hands clasped around her middle and brought it to his lips. "My dear, Lady Danby, my heart is incredibly happy to hear you say so. I have been uncertain if you held any tendre for me."

"I...I do admire you, my lord! Very much so, surely you suspected it."

"Please, call me Robert. And I could only hope, my dear."

"I...Robert, and you must call me Amelia."

They smiled at each other then fell into silence.

"This feels awkward—" the viscountess began.

"It does not have to be," his father interposed with earnest tenderness. "We are both pleased to see each other, let us accept the author of the note seems to suspect what is in our hearts."

"We do have a meddlesome matchmaker on our hands."

Graham glanced down at Miss Middleton, who seemed inordinately pleased her ruse was working. Except Graham felt as if the viscountess was perfectly aware of it and was doing a credible job of acting surprised. The deception affected Graham, and a heavy press of an unknown sensation lodged in his gut. His father deserved someone who held genuine affections for him, not a schemer out to snag herself an eligible, and very wealthy lord.

"Please see the mistletoe," Miss Middleton whispered.

The sound of his father's and Lady Danby's voices faded as he stared at the audacious minx before him.

"Oh, Mama, don't be shy," she whispered. "This is your chance!"

Anger curled through Graham at the lengths they would go to trap his father. No doubt his father thought the viscountess charming, as he had done with the other two charlatans who had only wanted his money. Graham glared at the back of Miss Middleton's head, despising that many ladies thought only of a man's wealth, and little of his character and his interests. He stepped closer to the deceptive minx. Her fragrance was clean and sweet, the fresh scent of lavender soap and roses. His heart jerked, and something unknown stirred inside him. He bit back a groan and tried to dismiss her from his awareness. It annoyed him he could feel attracted to this deceitful hoyden!

She softly clapped, and he glanced above her head. His father had held out his arm to the viscountess, and she was shyly holding onto his elbow. How demure and ladylike she seemed when she had plotted with her daughter for this outcome. Then, as if mischievous fairies worked with Miss Middleton, the sprig of mistletoe she had placed about the door dropped onto his father's head!

The earl reached for it, appearing bemused. Then he dipped his head and placed a passionate kiss on the viscountess's mouth. Miss Middleton gasped and covered her eyes. Graham stared at her in mute amazement. Blast his father for once again falling under the wiles of ladies who waged campaigns to steal into a man's life like they were generals on the battlefield. With single-minded concentration and absolute cunning.

"Robert!" the viscountess gasped breathlessly. "I... I...oh dear, this was so unexpected!"

"Oh, Mama, you can do it! You could be his countess if you would only dream a little," she urged in a whisper.

His irritation sharpened into something nearer to anger. Graham's heart grew colder, and he dipped his head and drawled right at her ear, "And I will do everything to ensure that my father does not marry that woman!"

A sharp gasp escaped Miss Middleton before she whirled around to face him. The prettiness of her features struck him, and he was speechless. Had he ever seen skin look that soft? She had pure creamy flesh with the lightest scattering of freckles across the bridge of a small nose. Tendrils of blonde curls rested becomingly on her forehead, and her gaze held such alarm he almost stepped back. An odd urge to lean in and kiss the top of her nose horrified him, and he scowled.

*Why is it the first woman I find attractive in years is this little schemer?*

Her golden-brown eyes glowed with secrets, mischief, and a good deal of ire. "You!"

He leaned in, so their lips were perilously close. Her breath hitched on a sharp inhale and her throat worked on a swallow.

"Yes...me!"

# CHAPTER 4

Callie froze where she stood, her heart a pounding roar in her ears. It was Viscount Sherbrooke. How handsome he appeared in dark trousers and jacket, with a burgundy waistcoat. His hair was messy and in need of taming. How rakish it made him look! He was one of the *ton's* most elusive marital catches, and the scandal sheets featured him often. With an effort of will, she maintained a serene expression. "I beg your pardon, Viscount Sherbrooke, I wasn't aware there was someone else here," Callie said with what she hoped was a great delicacy.

"Evidently," he said with an icy bite. "I believe you had preferred to conduct your outrageous plots in secrecy."

His stare was a tangible thing, reaching out to touch her. Yet it was not a tender look, something cold and judgmental filled his glare.

"Outrageous plots?" she asked softly. "What outrageous plot?"

His brow arched in sharp disbelief. "Ah, so even when caught you think to play the long game."

The door to the conservatory closed. She glanced over her shoulder, and noted her mother and the earl had left. Facing the viscount, she took a steady breath and lifted her chin to meet his unflinching and oddly intimidating regard.

"I am not playing any game."

She could see the dangerous glitter in his narrowed eyes, but she refused to give in to the urge to step back. Then his words came back to her. *And I will do everything to ensure that my father does not marry that woman!'*

"Whatever do you mean by saying you'll ensure your father does not marry my mother?" Callie demanded, thoroughly affronted.

"I believe I was clear, Miss Middleton. My father deserves more than a woman who would scheme with her daughter to entrap him," the viscount said in a voice mingled with civility and condescension.

"Mama has done nothing of the sort! And I only fanned the flame which had already been lit. A blind man could have sensed the attachment between the pair."

It galled Callie unspeakably that he might do something to rip apart her mother's happiness.

"And do you really think I would believe your mother had nothing to do with the contriving act you're putting on?" he drawled. "Spare me the act, I've gotten it enough times from fortune hunters looking to marry into our family's wealth."

She gasped, crushing the mistletoe between her fingers. "How dare you! My mother might endure strained circumstances, but she would never form an attachment with someone only because of money! There are genuine feelings, and I daresay Mama is falling in love."

"Love!" A sharp laugh which ended as soon as it began followed that incredulous utterance. His mien became even more remote, his eyes pinning her in place that of a hawk. It was positively uncomfortable.

"If the viscountess admires anything about Father, it is his deep pockets and connections."

She did not trust herself to make a civil reply. "You odious creature!" Well...she *did* try to hold her tongue for a few seconds. "Who gives you the right to object to true love?"

An arrogant brow lifted. "Ah...so your mother's feelings have even exceeded the normal type of affection? Of course, this..." he waved toward the mistletoe and the conservatory, and continued, scathingly, "This is *true love* and not the manipulation of a family after my family's fortune."

Callie faltered into astonishing stillness, an unknown tempest brewing in her breastbone. How had she ever thought this man handsome? He was the devil! For she could see he intended to ruin her mother's chance at happiness with the earl, and she would not allow it!

"I assure you, nothing of the sort is happening! I am appalled, mortified, and angry that you should think it and express your opinions in such an uncivil and arrogant manner. I cannot credit that the earl... who is kind and most thoughtful, is your father! I can see your purpose is to ruin my mother's chance at happiness, and I will not allow it," she fired, jabbing the point of her finger against his shoulder.

Surprise flared in his beautiful blue eyes before unexpected humor filled his gaze. The shift in his temperament rattled her.

"And how do you plan to stop me?" he asked with provoking amusement.

Sudden tears pricked behind her eyes, and her throat burned.

His eyes widened, and his entire body stilled. "Why are you crying?" he demanded in a gruff tone.

She fought her reaction with a will Callie hadn't known she possessed. It would be so mortifying if she should shed a tear in the odious man's presence. "I am not crying," she snapped, hating that her voice trembled.

"Then, what is this?"

The tender way he spoke had her peering into his eyes in surprise. He reached out, his thumb brushed against her cheek in a feather-light caress, and it was then she realized he traced the path of a tear. Her stomach twisted itself into a knot, and her breath hitched at the weakness that assailed her. "I have a tendency to express my emotions a bit too obviously."

"I supposed I frustrated you with my plans to thwart your schemes?" There was an edge of steel beneath the gentleness of his tone.

Her chest hurt with the effort to remain unaffected. "No...you do not know my mother...of her kindness, of her loyalty, and that when she loves, she does so with her entire heart. It hurts that you would judge her so unfairly and by the standards of other women you must have encountered in your life. I am not trying to entrap the earl. Never *that*."

She vibrated with indignation, took a deep breath, and continued, "I...I could see the tendre Lord Deerwood and my mother have for each other. Mama has been broken and hurt for so long, that it relieves my heart she still can love and yearn for more from life. My mama is pure of heart, demure, respectable, and though she is a bit enamored of scandal sheets, she is not mean-spirited at all! But she can be painfully shy, which some might misconstrue as indifference. I only thought to help her along, and it angers me you would try to take away the cheerful smile I just saw on her face because of your own arrogance and vanity. Your father is an earl...a man of maturity and excellent sense. I daresay he does not need you to decide whom he should shower with his attentions!"

He lowered his hands and studied her as if she were an unusual creature.

"You are very decided with your tongue, aren't you?"

Now he sounded as if he admired her.

"I agree, Miss Middleton, I do not know your mother, and I may do her a disservice by comparing her to others. I should also trust my father's judgment and not meddle in his affairs. I will endeavor to do so if you promise no more mischief."

She frowned. "I..."

He held up a hand. "*If* there is a genuine attachment between the pair, they will discover it for themselves with no added manipulation, wouldn't you agree?" he queried in a smooth voice, his eyes never leaving her face. "They've received a proper nudge just now...I am certain you also witnessed that passionate kiss."

She flushed, recalling the wicked embrace. She wondered if he was right, but Callie knew her mama. The viscountess would need several nudges, and while Callie's and Letty's encouragement were meant to be helpful, this dratted man would see it as manipulating his father. She wanted to growl at him. "I suppose so," she reluctantly agreed.

"And if love," he said with skepticism, "were to arrow its way into their hearts, it is up to the earl and Lady Danby to discover it with no one conspiring to set them up in a compromising situation that would lead to a forced marriage, especially with so many guests here. After all, there are many one notorious gossip amongst this set."

Oh! A revelation bloomed through her. "You do not believe in love," she said with soft surprise.

He jerked in surprise. "I love my family, and I know this because I would do everything necessary to protect them."

"There is also romantic love."

He grimaced. "I am sure there is," he said flatly. "It is not only his father who has been the recipient of many ladies' plot to align with my family. I still recall how unpleasant their cries of love were."

"I pity you since I believe you do not think love really exists. Not every wooing is about wealth and connections."

His face softened, and she was grateful for it.

"Ah...the flowers and the poetry, the lengthy walks and kissing, and then naked and sweaty, tangled limbs atop a bed? That is merely lust and a passion for life. If some want to call it love, who am I to object?"

Shock blossomed through her in a chilly wave. *Naked and sweaty, tangled limbs atop a bed?* The images provoked in her mind was salacious and downright shocking! Callie considered a variety of answers and rejected them all. What could she say?

Laughter and something devilish lurked in his brilliant eyes. "Ah..., I've distressed your sensibilities."

Callie retreated a few steps, needing the space between them, for his presence *was* overwhelming and, in that instant, felt wicked. The awareness they were alone...and that it was late, settled inside her. Instead of allowing her the distance, the dratted man followed her. She kept retreating, and he kept advancing. Callie only stopped when her rear encountered one of the Roman statues by the sashed windows.

"Miss Middleton...Callie..."

Her heart jerked at the intimacy of her name on his tongue.

"Is it a shortened name?"

"Yes," she husked. "Callisto..."

"Beautiful," he murmured, with a slight smile.

Why her father had decided to name her after a nymph, she had never understood.

Something indefinable gleamed in the viscount's gaze. "I cannot help noticing clenched between your fingers is a sprig of mistletoe."

With a sense of alarm, she glanced down at the small green leaves crushed in her hands. Callie released it as if it were fire, and it fell to the ground between them. She fought to gather her composure at their proximity.

"The mistletoe is still here...with us," he said with tender amusement.

"Oh dear," she said in a breathless gasp. Was he thinking of kissing her? *Surely not!* The uncomfortable sensation that he knew the errant path her thoughts had traversed assailed her.

Another gleam of humor appeared in his eyes. "Is that all you have to say?"

He held her hips and tugged her slowly to him, pressing her body against his. She should not let him hold her like this, yet unexpected anticipation sifted through her. She felt surrounded by a wall of muscles and warm skin. The thrill of something improper, unexpected, and wicked quivered through her. *I've never been kissed*, formed on her tongue, but what came out was, "I believe you are soon to announce an engagement with Miss Vinnette Brampton!"

Surprised flared in the gaze that stared down at her, then knowledge. "Ah, it was your footsteps I heard shuffling in the corridor last night."

*The rogue!* "My sister's," she husked.

"Miss Vinnette and I are friends. After she cried on my shoulder, I escorted her to her rooms safe and untouched."

Callie did not understand why she believed him or why such relief filled her veins with enough force to make her knees wobble. She did not even understand why she wasn't running from this situation. It felt reckless...and while she had a wild heart, she had never had a man stand this close to her before. And might very well never have it happen again. Within her an awful emptiness took root. *I am four and twenty, and I've never been kissed.* And weren't house parties the perfect occasions to be wicked and improper even if just only once?

He cupped her chin and lifted her face up to his regard. His gaze searched every nuance of her features as if he were trying to imprint something on his mind. "You are breathtakingly lovely," he murmured. "I do believe I even like your waspish tongue."

She gasped, torn between affront and amusement. "Why you—"

"It is my pleasure to divert your vexation," he said with a smile, brushing his thumb across her lower lip.

Her stomach fluttered as if it entrapped birds which were desperate to escape. There was something sinful in the gaze that stared at her lips as if he imagined her doing something terribly improper with her mouth.

A sweet ache trembled low in her belly.

*Oh...oh...oh!*

# CHAPTER 5

Graham dipped his head lower and claimed Callisto's lips before he could tell himself to fight the temptation. Her gasp of alarm allowed him entry, and he swept his tongue inside her mouth. She stiffened against him, and he gentled his kiss to soft, soothing nips, mindful of her delicate sensibilities. He pressed a series of light, teasing brushes of his mouth against hers. She opened herself to his persuasion, and with a sigh, she responded; he felt the inexperience, and inexplicably, it made him want her more.

She wilted against him, and ran her hands over his shoulders in a caress that felt as gentle as the brush of a butterfly's wing, to slip them around his neck. Then her response flamed with more hunger and the vivacity she had displayed earlier in their sparring.

Graham groaned and slanted her head, deepening

an already far too intimate kiss. Her innocent yet greedy response coaxing him to want more.

"You taste like heaven," he murmured.

She tipped on her toes and leaned into him even more. A soft moan echoed from her and vibrated through him. Desire erupted inside of him, and he wrapped her in an even closer embrace where the evidence of his desire would be unmissable.

She wrenched her lips from his, pressing trembling fingers to her mouth. "I did not expect that," she breathed. "Good heavens!"

"Neither did I."

She sent him a look of cool caution. "With a man of your varied experience, I doubt that mightily, my lord."

"It is because of my experience I can affirm I have never been lightheaded from a kiss before." Or so enthralled.

She gasped softly and her eyes widened.

How prettily she blushed. How furiously his heart pounded. From a mere kiss. He suspected it had everything to do with the lady before him. Her passionate defense of her mother and her unmistakable caring nature had filled him with surprised admiration.

Their gaze lowered to the mistletoe on the ground between them, before staring back at each other. A question lingered in her eyes, one that asked why he kissed her and what he meant by the intimate embrace. Graham could not answer, only knowing he wanted her in his arms again and her delightful mouth pressed against his. He reached for her and with another gasp she leaned back into the fountain.

*Bloody hell*. He was letting desire cloud his good judgement.

"Forgive me, I did not mean to frighten you. It will not happen again."

She dipped into a quick and graceless curtsy and then hurried away before he could gather his wits. He watched her retreating figure, wondering what the hell had just happened. While he'd had a few lovers over the years, he had never taken an innocent to his bed. He wasn't a rake or a man without honor or conscience. Lately, he had been thinking of setting himself up with a mistress, thinking it would be more convenient to have a woman ready whenever the urge rose to have some fun between the sheets. Graham had been moving slowly in procuring a *chère amie* because the idea of such an arrangement dissatisfied him.

There were days he hungered for someone to sit and talk with, for hours, perhaps about the work he was doing with his father or even find out about a woman's days and what her interests were. Then he imagined he could take that elusive someone to balls and carriage rides. In all honesty he had not thought a mistress would fill that role. And staring through the glass of the conservatory at Miss Middleton as she ran along the lantern-lit path to the main house, the awareness that the someone he'd been imagining felt remarkably similar to the lively and charming young woman who had just left his arms.

In that moment, the vague, shadowy figure who had been created in his most secret thoughts transformed into something tangible...and enchanting. *Bloody hell!* His knees wobbled, and he leaned against the statue. What was he saying? She was a lady, one with a respectable reputation. He could not dishonor or ruin her by asking her to be his mistress. She was fit for more than a quick romp beneath the sheets.

Simply put, Miss Middleton was a lady of quality and could only be taken as a wife.

*Sweet Christ.* Somehow, with the desire for more, which had been growing inside of him, he had never thought of settling down with a wife so soon. It was inevitable, but just not now! Perhaps after a few more years of enjoying his bachelorhood.

An intense awareness flowed through him. That said bachelorhood had bored him to hell, the clubs, and the fleeting lovers that only sated his lust but offered little else.

He scrubbed a hand over his face, and with a scowl, he made his way from the conservatory, determined to ignore his errant and unusual thoughts. It must be all the mistletoe sprigs around the manor and the jolly and hopeful atmosphere turning him to such sentimentality.

What else could it be?

. . .

THE FOLLOWING MORNING, Graham rode his horse, a massive black stallion, along the muddied lanes of the estate for an extended time, wanting to exhaust both himself and his horse. Outside, the day was bitter and gray, frosty morning mist crept over the land, and he inhaled the brisk, clean air into his lungs. He had dreamed of Callisto—of kissing her, of making love to her! He had jerked awake with his heart pounding to see the ash-gray rising dawn outside his windows and could not return to sleep. This was profoundly irritating. He'd not had a thought of her, even though he had known her to be his father's neighbor for over two years, but now she was a permanent fixture in his thoughts.

Slowing his horse, he guided the animal into a trot toward a small brook at the eastern section of the estate. There was not much snow on the ground, and so the brook should not be iced over. His horse could indulge in a drink and a rest before he took him back to the stables.

It didn't take long to reach, and once there, he dismounted and led Nightshine over to the bank where the horse drank from the icy stream. A rustle nearby had Graham shifting around where he spied his exquisite tormentor. She held something to her eyes and pointed in the distance toward the former groundskeeper's cottage. Then she pointed toward the lake and the sky, gesturing with animation to the lady beside her. Her sister, Miss Letitia, if he was not mistaken, vigorously shook her head, clearly objecting to whatever scheme Callisto plotted.

The pair of sisters could have come from some delightful illustration. Callisto fair in scarlet, and her sister's dark locks peeking from a fetching celestial blue bonnet that matched her bright blue pelisse. Against the backdrop of the snow-edged lake, the trees naked from their summer glory silhouetted in the dove-gray sky. Any artist would be enraptured and need to record the scene. Graham's heart leaped at the exquisite sight before him. Then he stomped on those thoughts, refusing to allow his creative inclination to deter him.

He walked toward them, ensuring his boots echoed upon the soggy ground. They whirled around, and Callisto's eyes widened when she saw him.

She averted her gaze before facing him with a militant glint in her compelling autumn eyes. Yes, she was indeed planning some misdeed.

"Up to more mischief, I see," he chided, staring at the spyglass in her hands.

She scowled in evident consternation, before dipping into a quick curtsey. "Lord Sherbrooke, how pleasant to see you up and about so early."

Her tone suggested she was everything but pleased.

The memory of their kiss lingered in her

thoughts, and a delightful blush reddened her cheeks. The answering jolt in his body was savage, and arousal curled through him. Her sister glanced between them, speculation heavy in golden-brown eyes much like Callisto's own.

"We were just admiring the sky," Miss Middleton murmured.

"And the cottage and the lake and our parents who are taking a morning stroll. I wonder what you could possibly be thinking," he said in a warning tone.

He would not let her off if she were plotting to use tricks to push his father toward her mother after their conversation last night.

She disarmed him with a grinned, surprising Graham. He had expected evasive stammers or something of the sort. Instead, she tossed her head and dared to wink.

"How wonderful you are not privy to my thoughts, my lord. If you will excuse us, Letty and I promised to join Lord Bybrook, Lord Duncan, and Miss Mary Peckham and Lady Shelby for a morning stroll."

Then she gripped her sister's hand and all but ran away. He stared bemused as she slipped in the mud, and her laughter floated on the air as she caught herself. Graham narrowed his eyes. He would need to observe Miss Callisto Middleton.

A fierce rush of pleasure filled him at the notion. He feasted his eyes on the delightful picture of her rear, despite the warm crimson pelisse that wrapped her slender form. His blood pumping fast as he remembered every single sensation of desire from squeezing that nubile body into his while he had ravished her with his kisses. Oh yes, he would enjoy keeping a close eye on that mischievous minx for the duration of the house party.

CHAPTER 6

His father's guests were having the time of their lives. The drawing room doors which led to the ballroom were opened and an orchestra set had been hired for tonight. Gentlemen and ladies dressed in their finery twirled about the ballroom with their dance partners, wide smiles on faces, facile chatter and laughter lingering on the air. It was not only the houseguest who were present at tonight's ball, but several neighbors with their daughters and sons had made the trek through the snow.

Graham had just finished partnering Lady Lizzie Morton with a waltz, and that young lady had batted her lashes and told him in no uncertain terms she would be married by next season. Not even in Town at the heights of the Season had he been on the receiving end of such unbridled flirtations. He blamed it on the mistletoe decorating the manor. It had encouraged normally sensible ladies and gentlemen to take leave of their senses.

His good friend Thomas Brampton currently danced the galop with Miss Middleton who was sheathed in a voluminous yellow satin gown which enhanced her frame exquisitely. Her loveliness as she smiled upon Thomas set Graham's heart to pounding and he glanced away feeling discomfited. He wasn't sure what he wanted from Miss Callie Middleton. He did not trust her intentions in regard to his father and believed her wholly capable of acting deceptively to trap his father. Yet he was attracted to her. Terribly so. His reaction unnerved him, simply for the fact he had never felt such a keen awareness before for a lady.

Wresting his attention from her, he made his way over to his father who lingered near the closed terrace windows, appearing miserable. Emma's hand rested his on his arm and she spoke to their father earnestly. She seemed to be offering him some encouragement. A quick scan of the room revealed the cause for that countenance. Lady Danby danced with Squire Brampton, and if Graham recalled correctly this was the second time she danced with the man since evening.

His father did not like that. To Graham's mind, the viscountess was keeping her options open. So much for Miss Middleton's assertions that her mother was falling in love.

"Who or what has put that scowl on your face?" Thomas asked, coming over to Graham.

He smoothed his expression into what he hoped was a serene countenance. "I thought you were occupied paying court to Miss Middleton."

Thomas smiled broadly. "She is a lovely creature to be sure, but it was only a dance. Alas she is not for me."

Graham arched a brow. "Too witty?"

Thomas scoffed. "That is not even the half of it, I fear she is even better read than I am and that my friend will not do. My wife will hang onto my sleeves, enraptured by my words. I fear Miss Middleton was hardly entranced with my retelling of the story of Hades and Persephone. The damn chit even corrected me at a few points."

Graham smiled, absurdly pleased, a state he was not willing to closely examine.

Thomas leaned in closer. "And the word about is that her family is broke."

Graham's gaze cut toward where she stood by the refreshment table with her sister. They were both glaring at their mother who now sat with a couple other ladies on chaise longue watching the dancers. His father had taken a young lady to the dance floor, but the viscountess did not look miserable. In truth she looked positively bored. Graham gritted his teeth. His father wore his heart on his sleeve for her while she appeared at best indifferent to his presence.

"Is that Viscount Worsley?" Thomas asked. "I am

astonished he could be parted from his gambling hell."

"He is recently married."

Thomas's jaw slackened. "Viscount Worsley *married*? I would more believe you saw a flying pig."

He chuckled understanding his friend's astonishment. The Viscount was known for his profligacy and wildness. The man owned one of the most notorious gambling *and* fighting club. "You should believe it. The news was all about Town only a few weeks ago."

"What is he doing here? I still owe his club several hundred pounds," Thomas muttered, tugging at his cravat, looking distinctly uncomfortable.

"They were visiting his wife's relatives in the area when their carriage damaged a wheel. They've put up here for the night while repairs are done."

Graham had been pleased to invite Worsley and his lovely wife, who had been thrilled to know of the soiree, to stay. "Lord Worsley said they will be moving on tomorrow. If you want to fall at his feet and beg for debt forgiveness, tomorrow morning would be the time."

A glance at Thomas revealed one of his hands pressed to his chest and his mouth parted in amazement. "Is *that* rather pretty creature his wife?"

Graham smiled. "That is his viscountess, yes."

A ravishing lady indeed with her midnight black hair piled high in a riot of curls atop her head, and her voluptuous figure draped in a silken dark green gown. Worsley led his wife to the dancefloor, and the way they peered at each other was almost embarrassing to observe. The man had a reputation of being wild and rakish where the *ton* had given him the moniker *'the wicked Viscount'*. Even when the newssheet had broken the news of his marriage, the headline had screamed: *The Sins of Viscount Worsley*, for it had astonished them a man of such profligacy had married a vicar's daughter. To see him now staring at his wife with such lascivious adoration filled Graham with a sense of longing. What would it be like to invest such feelings and attention into one person?

He allowed his gaze to stray to Miss Middleton. Graham stiffened. She was scampering out of the ballroom, casting determined glances at her mother and his father. *The minx!*

"Excuse me," he muttered to Thomas, and hurried after her without being too obvious. The last thing he wanted was for the guests to speculate on their joint disappearances.

He caught up to her just as she entered the library and shut the door behind her. Opening it silently, he closed it with a *snick* and leaned against the door. She sat in his father's chair and opened the top drawer, rifling the content.

"Up to more mischief I see," he murmured. "This I believe calls for some sort of punishment."

Graham admired her composure. She did not scream even though her alarm was evident.

Lowering the hand pressed over her chest, she said, "You!"

"Yes, *me*. Must we always meet like this, hmm?"

She closed the drawer and narrowed her eyes at him. "Did you follow me?"

"Of course."

"And whatever did you mean by 'this calls for punishment'. Surely you jest."

Abandoning her scheme, Miss Middleton stood and sauntered toward him. Her scent of lavender and something mouthwatering and elusive assailed his senses. *Sweet Mercy*. "Were you not reneging on our agreement?"

Delicate brows arched. "I was about to pen a note and you interrupted."

"A note to our parents."

A heavy fringe of sooty lashes framed her golden-brown eyes enchantingly. Those lashes now fluttered innocently at him. "Of course not."

"Liar," he said with some amusement, irritated with himself to find anything humorous in her reactions. "You were going to send some message that would have them scrambling like puppets to meet each other in some secret place."

Her face flushed so becomingly. "I'll never own that was my intention."

Something suspiciously like amusement colored her tone.

Graham scoffed. "Of course not." Would she ever stop her meddling ways?

"Your mother remains indifferent to my father, why do you persist in playing the matchmaker?"

"You do not know her like I do. She...mama is not indifferent, I assure you. She has guarded her heart very well after papa's death, but it comes alive for Lord Deerwood."

His heart jolted. "You are a romantic."

"Unapologetically," she said with a sweet smile.

"Would you honor me with a dance, Miss Middleton?"

The request startled them both.

One hand pressed against her chest, and the more she stared at him the wider her lovely eyes got. "Here?"

"No."

Amusement softened her lips. "Then where?" she asked softly, looking at him as if she were trying to decipher a puzzle.

"In the ballroom."

She gave him an assessing glance, then lifted her chin a notch. "There will be much speculation should we return together."

Suddenly hating the distance between them, he pushed from the door and in three strides he was right there. Close enough where he could touch her.

Her lips parted as she stared up at him, her breath hitching with a noisy inhale.

"Perhaps at the next soiree then."

"Yes," she said on a swallow. "At the next one."

"Callie?"

She blushed at the intimate use of her name. "Yes?"

"I am on to you and for the rest of the house party...I will not let you and your mischief out of my sight. Whatever you are planning, you can forget about it now."

She gasped her outrage and he dipped his head and caught it with his mouth. With a muffled groan, she tipped onto her toes and arched into him, opening her mouth for the demanding sweep of his tongue against the seam of her lips. He groaned at the sweet taste of her.

The kiss ended as suddenly as it began when she wrenched her mouth free of his with a startled yet very aroused gasp. Her fingers came up to her lips, which were reddened and swollen from his kiss. He couldn't apologize for it, not when kissing her had been in his thoughts for several hours, not when her lips had haunted him all of last night. The memory of the feel of her body against him, the taste of her, the little sounds she'd made when he had scandalously touched his tongue to her lips. That hot whimper had tormented him even his dreams.

"I should apologize but it would make me a hypocrite."

"What are your intentions?" she asked with a voice that trembled. "Why...why do you kiss me?"

"I have none," he said with a touch of regret.

She chuckled, shaking her head in amused disbelief. "You rogue! Keep your mouth to yourself."

Now it was her voice that seemed shaded with regret and longing.

He scrubbed a hand over his face. She was right. He was acting the rogue. If he wanted her, he should damn well court her. Except he wasn't certain he wanted her beyond the raw, physical attraction he felt.

He should be treading with caution; instead he was being reckless. Scowling at his undisciplined reactions, he bowed, turned and left the library before he did something foolish like kiss her without thoughts of consequences or of tomorrow.

CHAPTER 7

olliwell Manor was a majestic three-story
building set in exquisite landscaped grounds.
The house built to replace a less prestigious building
was elegant and classical in design. Each elevation
was majestic and fitting to the local scenery. The
grounds were equally splendid, although the formal
gardens could not be seen at their best at this time of
year as few flowers blossomed. However, Callie could
imagine it as a riot of colors in summer. Then the
fountains, artfully placed statuary of ancient gods and
goddesses, would be surrounded by leafy bowers and
exotic flowers.

There were pretty walks through the woodland
interspersed with several well-placed gazeboes and
some accurate recreations of ruins. The house had a
wonderful conservatory and several greenhouses
where fruit and flowers could be grown out of season.
And despite the grandness of the estate she could not

seem to escape the viscount. He shadowed her every move and he did it in such an innocent manner it appeared a coincidence. But Callie knew better. He did not trust her to leave their parents alone to find each other.

A sinking sensation formed in the pit of Callie's stomach. There really was no way to convince him she was not being mischievous. *Drat!* She scowled at the alarming and improper way he shadowed her for the entire morning. Surely people would start to think his behavior peculiar. Worse, she did not want to think about the way he had kissed her in the conservatory and then last night in the library.

The rogue was getting bolder and she would be a liar if she claimed to hate his attention. Something wicked had bloomed inside of her with that first kiss. And then last night. Callie had dreamed of being kissed senseless, of being ravished and held in the viscount's wicked embrace. She closed her eyes against the memories, but they came, uncaring of her resolve to forget the viscount.

She gave her head a swift shake before her thoughts took her any farther down that scandalous and wanton memory. Everything must be about her mother and the earl finding their hearts with each other. Not the impossible attraction she felt for the man's son. The Viscount had been playing billiards with Mr. Thomas Brampton earlier, and as soon as the young Lord Sherbrooke spied her, he had abandoned the man and the game to observe her.

Shameful and outrageous! And worse, she blushed like a silly miss whenever their gazes collided.

The memory of his kisses lingered in the air once they looked at each other. She swore every time she felt his stare, and whenever she returned his regard that wicked knowledge shone from him, and she would become warm and out of sorts in so many wretched ways.

A panting Letty hurried over to her. "It is done! Mama is now by the lake, and I slipped the note beneath the earl's door. Surely he will meet her there soon."

"Hush," Callie said, glancing to see how close the viscount stood.

She did not turn around, but she anticipated Viscount Sherbrooke to be right behind her.

"Why are you whispering?" Letty demanded.

"I do not wish Viscount Sherbrooke to know what we are doing."

"Are you certain the viscount is following you?" Letty asked, her eyes laughing. "I think your imagination is running amok! I daresay he does not notice us at all."

Interest flashed in her sister's eyes. "I knew it! You blushed frightfully yesterday morning when you saw him. How is he aware of our antics?" her sister's elegant brow winged upward. "Callie...are you blushing *again*?"

With a scowl, she grabbed her sister's arm and tugged her toward an unoccupied gazebo. She smiled politely at the few gentlemen and ladies strolling about. The morning was unexpectedly warm, but she sensed it would not last long, for she could see the rain clouds in the far-off distance. And her plan hinged on that rain actually appearing.

"Will you tell me what happened with the viscount, or am I left to guess?"

Looking about to ensure they had cleared all listening ears, she muttered, "He kissed me."

Letty faltered, forcing Callie to stop.

"Twice."

"He kissed you...*twice?*"

"Yes."

"Where?"

Callie rolled her eyes. "On my shoulder."

"Upon my word! Why would he—"

"Letty, for heaven's sake! I was funning you," Callie said, then lowered her voice to say, "he kissed my mouth and I...I kissed him back. In truth I have been able to think of little else."

"Oh, my."

*Oh, my indeed.*

"Do you like the viscount? Because I do not think you can marry him and then his father marry mamma. Is that...is that even legal?"

She flushed hot, and annoyance prickled her spine. "Letty you go too far. It was just a few kisses and you are suggesting marriage! I do not even like him!"

Her sister folded her arms beneath her bosom and

arched an elegant brow. "Then why did you allow him liberties?"

Callie closed her eyes briefly. "I...I feel a bit foolish to say this but when he kisses me, I feel like he is the center of a storm and I am happy to be caught in it." An odd sensation quivered low in her belly.

Letty appeared at loss for words for several seconds, then said, "Is he courting you?"

"He has no favorable intentions." And Callie did not know if she wanted him to have any.

In round-eyed astonishment, her sister glared at her. "That leech! Ruining Vinnette did not satisfy—"

"He did not ruin her," Callie blurted, disconcerted by how she wanted to defend him. Did she dare to really like the viscount?

"Oh," Letty said, her ire deflated. "Still...what did he mean by his kisses?" she asked with naïve curiosity.

Callie lifted a shoulder in a shrug, not wanting to admit she had wondered the same thing for hours. Was he interested in her, or was he playing the libertine? "I do not want to think about that *now*...we need to direct all our efforts to Mama. She was refusing to come down this morning for fear of encountering the earl."

"Yes, I heard all those mutterings about the dreadful mistake she made. It took much convincing for her to accept the earl's invitation to a stroll this morning," Letty said with a heavy sigh. "Why did he not asked her to dance at last night's soiree. It is evident the earl is shamelessly besotted. He danced with three ladies and not once with mamma. She was miserable for it."

"I think mamma is being too careful with her emotions, it makes her seems rather indifferent. Perhaps Lord Deerwood was uncertain. But he tried to make up for it this morning. We did shamefully eavesdrop, and the earl worked hard to persuade Mama to take a stroll with him," Callie replied, wondering for the first time if she should allow the entire scheme to run its course naturally as the viscount suggested.

Then she recalled how delighted her mother had seemed before she'd allowed the fear to burrow into her heart. But what did she fear? "Letty...do you think Mama is afraid to love again?"

Letty swallowed, a shadow of pain darkening her eyes. "We all still miss Papa so dreadfully. Perhaps she is afraid. Mama did just now inform us we will quit the house party early!"

They shared a speaking glance, and said in unison, "She is running!"

Callie worried her bottom lip with her teeth. She wouldn't want her mama to live with guilt about betraying Papa, and if there was a chance of that happening, then she may truly not be ready for a new love.

"Oh Letty, I have been so single-mindedly concentrated on securing Mama's happiness, I never truly expected that she would resist the earl when she so plainly admires him. We must put a stop to the rowing!"

Letty nodded, and they hurried across the too-large lawns toward the lake in the distance. As they approached, she spied her mother peering up at the earl, a frown on her face. The man only seemed besotted while her mother appeared cautious.

"Mama," Callie cried, pressing a hand atop her head to secure her bonnet under the sharp gust of wind.

Their mother turned and waved, a smile lighting her face. Their mother was still an extraordinarily gorgeous woman, without a hint of gray in her vibrant mass of primrose-colored hair. Her eyes were a pale green, and her figure had retained its elegant slenderness. As they drew closer, Callie spied the viscount ambling toward them from the impressive stables. He was devilishly handsome in an open black great-coat thrown over his dark blue jacket, gray waistcoat, dark trousers, and the *de rigueur* white shirt and cravat. His ebony hair was well groomed, and his beautiful dark blue eyes quickly scanned her body.

Her breath hitched and she gasped as mortification raced through her heart. Thankfully, she had worn her best gown today with a green redingote and a stylish matching bonnet. She knew she was fetching to look at, and the appreciative glint in his eye warmed her. Callie dearly hoped her attraction to the man wasn't visible for all to see.

Worse, she did not want him to now believe she was trying to set her cap for him!

She hurried her steps, wanting to reach her mama and save her from falling into the plot before the viscount arrived. But the wretched man increased his pace to match her strides. They arrived at their parents on the verge of breaking into all out sprints, as he blurted, "What a charming coincidence to find you here, Miss Middleton."

Callie's thoughts churned, and she glared at the viscount. "I was about to see if Mama wanted to play croquet with a few of us by the eastern side of the lawns."

"The grounds are wet," the earl inserted. "I would not recommend it."

"Yes, and Lord Prescott is urgently searching for you, Father. Something about the news of an investment you are both a part of."

The earl started in surprise. "He is?"

"Quite so," the viscount drawled.

Callie gaped at him, suspecting that he fibbed. Her ire rose, for he was intent on sabotaging whatever he thought she planned.

"Robert..." her mother began, "Oh! I meant to say, Lord Deerwood, please attend to your business."

Her mother failed to hide her deflation, and it made Callie realize that her mother's desire for happiness may outweigh the fears which drove her earlier to decide to flee the house party. The nudge toward her heart's desire was still needed.

The earl seemed crestfallen. "I do suppose we could row on the lake another time, Lady Danby."

Callie touched their mother's hand. "Mama, you've wished so very much to row—"

"And father has been telling me how much he wished for news on the copper mines he's invested in. Surely the rowing can wait."

"The boats are already prepared," Callie interposed.

She glared at him and fought not to squirm under the intensity of his stare.

"And Lord Prescott is waiting," the viscount drawled.

Their parents' gazes volleyed between them, and they shared a glance Callie could not interpret. Letty seemed amused and did nothing to hide her reaction.

Her mother chose that instance to say, "I do know you also enjoy rowing, my dear. Why don't you take the boat out with the viscount? I did not sleep well last night, and I fear it has brought on a mild headache. I should rest before it becomes a greater discomfort."

"Yes, I would be honored to show you the lake, Miss Middleton," the viscount said, amusement dancing in his eyes. "I am sure it will be a relaxing endeavor."

Callie swallowed the sound of outrage welling in her throat. It wouldn't do for anyone to see how much he annoyed her. Her mother turned bright, curious eyes to her, and a heaviness settled in Callie's stomach. There would be no getting her mama and the earl into the boat now. Perhaps the rain would not come at all, and her twitching nose had been an anomaly.

"Perhaps for a few minutes, I believed rain might come soon," she said, admitting that her agreement was because she wanted to spend a few minutes with the viscount.

Callie had never been the sort of person to shy away from complicated situations, she preferred to understand them, and the curious sensations stirring in her heart caused by the viscount warranted close examination.

"Oh, my daughter has a nose for sensing the rain," the viscountess said with an airy laugh. "It is indeed fascinating."

"How curious then she would want you to be caught in the rain, my lady," Graham speculated, his cynical eyes pinning her.

She refused to squirm. Callie couldn't very well admit that she had been hoping the rain would trap their parents once they've reached the far end of the lake. That would violate the agreement between her and the viscount. Dusk would arrive, and with the rains, it would be impossible to return, and they would be forced to spend the night in the cottage she and Letty had painstakingly arranged to be aired and cleaned!

A few minutes later, she sat comfortably in the rowing boat with the viscount. Her mother, Letty, and the earl had waved them off before walking away. Now that she was alone with the man, an unexpected wave of shyness consumed Callie. The silliness of it made her frown several times, and the dratted man did not help by staring at her. His powerful shoulders lifted as he clawed back the oars taking them across the wide picturesque lake.

"I do not think we should go too far," she warned.

He glanced at the sky. "I doubt we have much to worry about."

"Do not be deceived by the sun, my nose has been twitching!"

That drew a smile from him. "Twitching?"

"Yes. I could be reading or taking a stroll or eating breakfast with my family, and my nose just moves on its own. It smells or senses the rain."

He cast her an arresting glance. "I find that notion alarming. An appendage taking on a life of its own."

Callie surprised them by laughing. "It really confounds my family. But I can always tell when it is about to rain. Perhaps my nose is enchanted."

"Ah, it's not just your nose I'm afraid," he muttered as if bemused.

She flushed and dared a glance at him, and found not a trace of humor on his face. *He finds me enchanting.*

"What do you enjoy besides playing matchmaker, Callisto," he said, and it was as if he savored the sound of her name on his lips. "I find I am very curious about you."

A sharp breath burned in her throat at the way his gaze moved over her but did not look away. "I very much enjoy reading."

"Ah, yes...I had the pleasure once of watching you for several minutes. You were so engrossed you did not sense my presence."

She clasped her gloved hands in her lap, recalling the encounter, and how rude she'd thought him at the time for walking away without murmuring a greeting.

"I admire that you do nothing half measure," he said.

Surprise jolted through Callie. Her father had repeated a similar refrain several times to her. "Why would you think I did not?" she enquired, her voice shaking.

"When I watched you read with your entire face and heart. I felt the passion you saw in your book. I knew when your characters were happy or sad. Everything about you was immersed. I daresay even your will to push your mother into the path of my father speaks to your character. The way you responded to my kisses..."

She gasped, her heart beating just a little bit faster. "Lord Graham!"

"There was no shyness when I coaxed your lips to part for me. No fright when I touched my tongue to yours. You hurtled towards the desire sweeping through you...and I can tell how you would approach everything with such unrestrained passion. Whether it be reading, dancing, riding a horse, playing matchmaker, or...kissing."

A crack of thunder saved her from replying. Though she couldn't imagine what she might have said. The sky opened, and rain fell in torrents.

He started rowing the boat toward the bank closest to them but paused after glancing behind her. Callie knew what he had spied. The cottage.

*Dear God! Not the cottage!*

"We should head back to the estate," she cried out.

"You'll catch your death by the time we reach back there," he said, grunting with the effort to row as fast as he could toward the embankment leading to the cottage.

With a sense of shock, she realized she had fallen into the trap of her own making. What would the viscount say...or do when he saw what awaited them inside the cottage?

CHAPTER 8

It was a mad dash through the rain, and Graham held onto Miss Middleton's hand as she slipped in the mud. He caught her, and the blasted woman laughed, lifting her face to the rain. Her bonnet was soaked, and she already appeared like a drowned rat. If he had taken several minutes to row them back to the estate, surely, she would have drowned in the deluge.

He tugged her forward. To their misfortune, the cottage had been unoccupied for several months and should be dusty and uncomfortable. He hoped there was no roof leakage. An ominous rumble of thunder shook the sky, and he feared they were in for a winter squall. They clambered up the slight steps, wrenched the door open, and spilled into shocking warmth. Graham's steps faltered, and he looked down at her. Miss Middleton withdrew her hand from his and stared up at him with wide eyes.

"You have been rather busy with your mischief, Miss Middleton," he murmured, surveying the exceptionally tidy and toasty room which held a roaring fire. "It seems there is no end to your deception."

Her affected serenity was momentarily ruffled, then she rallied and replied, "Not deception, surely, it is more gentle encouragement. Quite a different thing altogether, I am certain you would agree."

He swore under his breath. "Is that the distinction you used to justify your action?"

She pursed her lush lips. "Yes."

*Shameless minx!*

The interior of the cottage chased away the chill from the rain, and it had been recently aired and cleaned. The scent of lemon wax was redolent on the air. Pinecones, evergreens, and mistletoes decorated the tight room, and there were fresh linens on the bed. Surprise jerked through him when he noted the carafe of wine on a small table by the windows. There seemed to be marzipan, gingerbread, and cake as well on a large white platter. *Good God.*

"However did you get the servants to go along with this madness?" They must have questioned her intentions and gossiped amongst themselves.

"My papa usually lamented that I was a silver-tongued devil," she said with a quick smile and her usual buoyancy. "But I conveyed that these orders were"—her eyes flitted everywhere but at him —"from...*you.*"

Her impudence knew no bounds.

She strolled over to the hearth, and untied her bonnet, then rested it on the mantle. Then she tugged off her coat and gloves, placing them on the grate near the fire. She did not appear as wet as he'd imagined, but her dress clung in a few damp places. She kneeled and removed her half-boots, revealing white silken stockings. She stood, faced him, then lifted her chin in challenge as if to say, 'I did it and there is *nothing* you can do.'

Something primal in his gut stirred, a direct response to that defiance.

Humor lit in her expressive eyes, and her lips curved. "I can see that you want to roar but you are restraining yourself. How admirable that you are not a gentleman to give in to excessive display of emotions."

How utterly delightful she looked, and he did not miss the guilty flush on her cheeks. Yet he was not angry.

"I am not angry." Mystifying indeed.

"I am glad to hear it," she said softly.

He walked over to the fire, never taking his eyes from her. He shrugged from his wet jacket and removed his waistcoat, then also removed his boots, which felt waterlogged.

Her lips parted, and she bit her bottom lip, a nervous gesture, but one that set his heart to pounding. He noted the sprigs of mistletoe and berries hanging from the roof by lengthy pieces of ribbons. She had apparently hoped her mother would be ravished, and Graham knew if his father had ended up here with Lady Danby, what Miss Middleton hoped for would have happened.

*The scheming, mischievous minx*, he thought a bit too fondly.

"You do realize no matter where you are in this cottage, you will be under a mistletoe," he murmured soft and wicked.

A becoming flush crept up her slender neck, pinkening her fair cheeks. She grasped something from the mantle, and he noted it was a deck of cards.

"How thoughtful of you to provide some entertainment beyond debauchery," he mocked.

She cast him a wide-eyed glance. "*That* was never my intention."

"Your delightful nose warned you of rain, and you ruthlessly conspired to have two people alone so far away from the estate trapped here. No one will come looking since this squall seems like it will last the rest of the evening, and everyone should be too busy with the planned entertainment to worry about any missing party members. Well played, Miss Middleton, *well played*."

He spread his hands wide. "Except, it is me you have gotten here, and I wonder if I should fear for my virtue. You are an odd and improper sort of lady; I cannot fathom your intentions."

She folded her hands about her middle, canted her head, and stared at him. Though she tried to appear nonchalant, her lovely eyes danced with mirth. "I never expected us to end up here, Viscount Sherbrooke."

"Nonsense! You should have convinced me more about the wonders of your twitching nose. Now for the next few hours, I shall live in fear of ravishment."

She giggled, and the sweetness of the sound burrowed into his heart and filled him with a peculiar but welcoming warmth.

She batted her lashes. "You need not fear debauchery from me, Viscount Sherbrooke, I promise your virtue will be intact when we leave here. I will conduct myself most admirably!"

He wanted her. A few kisses, but it would be most difficult to prevent himself from doing more...and there was no understanding between them. Perplexingly, he found himself wanting to make promises. Graham want to woo her and get to know every wonderful detail about Miss Callie Middleton. He governed his needs, for he was not rash in his behavior but meticulous and pragmatic. Yet, she inspired his heart to throw caution to the winds! "Ah...pity that, however, I shall practice gentlemanly restraint."

Her red, delectable lips formed an 'O.'

"Whatever shall we do to pass the time?" he crooned, shifting closer to her.

She blushed, wrinkled her nose before gracing him with another pretty smile. "Perhaps we could read or play cards...or just talk. I am frightfully curious about you and have been for some time."

It was then he noted a few leather-bound volumes atop the mantle. It seemed she had planned a non-lustful manner of entertainment for their parents. *How innocent*. "I am curious about you as well."

She sent him a saucy wink. "Mutually assured madness is always welcome."

Bloody hell, he *was* charmed.

"We've been neighbors for a while but have hardly crossed paths." This bit she admitted shyly.

"I do not live here at Holliwell Manor. I recently bought a townhouse and a country estate with some investments, which gave me handsome returns."

"Those properties are not entailed to the earldom?"

"No, I must plan for the eventuality of having more than one child. I would like to afford my daughters or second son with more opportunities than the army or the clergy."

Mischief danced in her eyes. "Oh, la-la! So, you *do* plan to marry."

"Eventually. I know my duty."

"Is that all marriage is to you? Duty? What about love?" she questioned.

He lifted a shoulder in an indifferent shrug. "It is not a requirement for marriage."

She scoffed. "I daresay it should be!"

"Why?"

"Surely you jest?"

"I never do about matters of the heart."

They sat before the small table, and he poured wine in two glasses. She took the drink he handed to her and sipped appreciatively.

"At least you will admit to having a heart."

He chuckled, genuinely enjoying her rejoinders.

She peered at him over the rim of her wine glass. "Can you imagine spending the rest of your life with a woman you barely liked? Though I wish to marry and have my own home, it would mortify me to marry a gentleman I did not esteem. How can you think to marry without sentiments?"

No, he could not imagine a cold union without affections. His parents had loved each other dearly, and it had almost broken his father when she died. Still, the earl had rallied and was ardently pursuing another union.

"So you wish to marry," he murmured.

"I daresay I do!"

"Then, why are you still unwedded?" he asked, wondering if there was something more to it than her lack of dowry.

She hesitated to reply, taking several sips of her wine as if to gather her thoughts. Callisto lowered the glass, and he grabbed the carafe and topped it up.

"I suppose no gentleman of the *ton* is interested in a young lady with little connections and no money. It would take a rare man to look beyond such deficiencies, and where would I find such a man? Certainly not here in Gloucestershire. I've been slowly losing my faith that love is all that is required, and I must perhaps accept I am destined to remain a spinster."

She seemed embarrassed by her frankness and took a few hurried gulps of her wine.

"And what is your idea of the perfect partner?" he asked, lazily sipping his wine, watching each shift of her animated expressions.

"That he loves me. And that is he kind, considerate...tender and playful."

Incredulity rushed through him. "That is it?"

"Are those not the best of qualities?" she demanded, looking affronted.

"There are greater considerations to the matter."

She arched a delicate brow. "Such as?"

"You should require that your beau possesses enough wealth to keep you in pretty dresses and fancy carriages. A townhouse in London, fashionable balls and routs, and a few country homes here and there? My dear, Callisto, love cannot provide for you and any children you might have! You have to be more practical than romantic when hoping for a suitor."

She had the gall to roll her eyes. "Of course, I wish to be comfortable, and for my husband to be able to provide for his family. But I would prefer to wed a man who loves me with every emotion in his heart than a duke who can lavish me with clothes, homes, and diamonds but does not love me."

She set her elbows onto the table and rested her

chin on her palm. "The ideal partner could love me *and* be wealthy!" Then she winked at him. "A man such as yourself, but you must be persuaded that sentiments between lovers are as necessary as breathing air!"

Graham laughed, delighted with her. "And how would you convince me of this?"

An unexpected silence fell between them, and her gaze lingered on his lips for shocking moments.

"With kisses perhaps," she whispered, a crooked smile curving her lips. "You were my first."

Astonishment had him stiffening. "Your first what?"

Their gazes collided and held for a moment.

"To kiss me," she whispered.

Something hot and primal stirred in his gut. "I hope I did not disappoint." The remarkably intimate nature of their conversation did not escape his awareness.

"Are you fishing for flattery?"

"A gentleman's vanity needs to be stroked occasionally," he murmured, never taking his eyes from her smile. His heart pounded in a manner he did not understand and may never do.

"I daresay it was beyond wonderful." Callisto lowered her eyes and blatantly pretended to be intrigued by the array of cakes and gingerbread on the platter. Except the tip of her ears and her cheeks burned a bright red.

Everything inside of Graham collapsed. *And I feel*

*like I want to be your last.* Yet he did not say it, instead he plucked one of the titles she had selected—*Emma,* by Jane Austen, opened the pages and read. With a jubilant sigh, she placed both elbows on the table and popped a piece of gingerbread in her mouth, thoroughly immersed in the story he narrated. At times she gasped and held her breath as if she were the one reading. Knowing he had such a captivatingly rapt audience, Graham did something he'd never done before—changed his voice to reflect each character.

This brought such laughter from her, and it rang in the cottage suffusing him with joy.

"Good heavens," she said, still chuckling. "I know no female who speaks with such a high squeal. I am affronted on behalf of my sex!"

Never had he felt contentment equal to the sensations blossoming through his heart. They ate, read, and laughed. Of course, she gobbled the cakes and gingerbread as she did everything—with zest and her entire heart.

They argued about the last piece of cake which ended with it being shared. He told her of the motions he assisted his father in writing for Parliament, the countless hours of research and preparation it took, and sometimes the worry he felt about whether he would acquit himself honorably to the earldom when he inherited.

*"You will!"* She had reassured him so ardently. *"I can see your mettle...it is one of strength and honor."*

What did he like—horses, restoring a beautiful home, especially if it retains signs of its Tudor architecture, and reading. How happy that had made her for they now had a common interest and the best of them all—reading, declaring that, 'inside the pages of every book was a whole other world that she could get lost in'.

She also enjoyed dancing. Though she had never danced the waltz despite having learned the steps and form from her papa. During her first and only Season in London, her father had fallen ill, and she had returned to Suffolk, where they had resided. After they had completed the mourning period, she, along with her mother and sister, had to leave their beloved homes so a distant cousin could inherit. There had been no money or time for another Season, as they had directed their efforts on keeping their heads above water without losing their reputations.

As she recounted the tale candidly, Callisto hadn't seemed to resent her situation but appeared as a woman who understood life at times threw brutal punches, and it was the character of the person which determined if they stayed on the ground or sprung back up with lively purpose.

His admiration for her grew then, and as if it were the norm, he lowered the book, walked around to her chair, dipped into a bow, held out his hand, and said, "Might I have your hand for a dance, Miss Middleton?"

With a wide smile on her lips and merriment

glowing from her lovely eyes, she nodded. Now she was in his arms, and the intent way she peered up at him evoked confusing feelings inside him. He wanted to ravish and protect her in equal measures. The duality of those needs clashed painfully inside of him. *I've never felt this way about a lady before*, he wanted to confess. But it seemed premature to do so. What if this warm sensation did not last but faded like ashes in the wind once he was apart from her?

"Sadly, there is no music," he said.

The longest of lashes flickered, and she peered up at him. "The rain and thunder will do."

A quick ripple of laughter escaped her as he spun her in a twirl, humming the tune for them.

"Oh, Graham, this is simply wonderful!"

The sound of his name on her lips did marvelous things to his heart. It flipped several times as if it too danced.

"We are standing below mistletoe berries," he said, bringing them to a stop in the center of the room.

"I fear the servants went a bit overboard in their enthusiasm. We cannot escape them, it seems."

He skimmed his fingers over her cheek, almost tentative in his exploration. Then he gave in to the clamor in his heart, lowered his head and pressed a kiss to the corner of her lips.

# CHAPTER 9

The rain sleeted down and rattled the door and the small window of the cottage, but she felt frightfully warm. Held tenderly against the Viscount's chest Callie felt as if she was caged within her own storm—one of brilliant fire and the hottest delight. Graham's kiss was light, tender, sweet, and her heart tumbled over inside her chest.

"What was that for?" she whispered against his mouth.

"There *are* mistletoe sprigs all over this cabin," he replied with gentle amusement. "Wasn't this the idea when you had them placed?" He possessed such a confident presence that appealed to her beyond measure.

Callie blushed but held his stare. "I meant them for your father, and my mother."

"Then let's move away."

He twirled her off in another direction and then glanced up. "Alas, another one."

This time he pressed a kiss atop her nose, and she laughed lightly, dizzy with the heat pouring through her. The last two hours with him in the cabin had revealed a charming and good-natured gentleman that made her yearn for impossible dreams.

He spun with her again, and when he paused, they both looked up.

"Yet more mistletoe," she said with a wide smile, but how her heart pounded.

"Did you know it is widely believed that it was the Norsemen and women who first romanticized mistletoe?"

"I did not know that," she said with a small smile. "But I knew the Celtic druids used it for vitality and fertility."

"Hmm." His fingers brushed against the fluttering pulse at her throat, lingering there too long to be an accident. "In Norse mythology, when Odin's son Baldur was prophesied to die, his mother Frigg—the goddess of love—went to all the animals and plants of the earth to secure an oath that they would not harm her son. But Frigg neglected to consult with the unassuming mistletoe, so the scheming Loki made an arrow from the plant and saw that it was used to kill the otherwise invincible Baldur. The gods were able to resurrect Baldur from the dead to his mother's delight. The goddess of love then declared mistletoe a symbol of love and vowed to plant a kiss on all

STACY REID

those who passed beneath it. That folklore evolved where we fine gentlemen are encouraged to steal a kiss from any woman caught standing under the mistletoe and refusing is viewed as bad luck."

He touched her elbow, urging her to him, yet his clasp felt gentle and protective.

The thrill he gave Callie amazed her. "I would hate to deny you and endure any misfortune," she teased.

His dark eyebrows arched, then he spoke in a velvet murmur, "How you delight my heart just now."

He lifted her chin with a finger. Whenever his blue gaze met hers, her heart turned over in response. Callie's whole being seemed filled with waiting. His thumb swiped over her lips. The caress was a command. And she parted her lips.

His head reached down, and Graham kissed her mouth more persuasive than she would have liked to admit. Wicked heat darted through her wanton heart, and she slipped her hands around his neck and held him to her. He tasted like a summer storm, he tasted like happiness...and ruin. They spoke of no sentiments, nor had he made any promises, yet Callie was helpless against the desires sweeping through her body.

*I am four and twenty...whenever am I going to burn with need like this in someone's arms.*

He plundered to her mouth, stroking her tongue with his. Their kiss was fiery, wild, and wet. *Oh, God.* It was as if she was another person. Excitement

84

hummed in her veins, and everything that had been wrong and uncertain, righted itself.

*How was this possible?*

He stole the rest of her thoughts with his drugging kisses, and she moaned as arousal stirred in her blood. His lips searched a path down her neck, her shoulders, and to the top of the lace that protected her breasts from his ravishment. Graham recaptured her lips, more demanding this time, and she responded with a flaming passion.

She distantly became aware he removed her clothes, and they fell away from her body. Her dress, chemise, laces, and corset were removed with kisses in between. Then she was in his arms being carried over to the small bed flush against the corner wall opposite the fire. It was a little darker there, but she could see the possessive glint in his beautiful eyes, the raw hunger surrounding her like a caged storm waiting to be unleashed. And she was not afraid. She wanted this to fill all the places that had hungered for so many things but had remained unfulfilled. He bore her down on the bed, then moved away to remove the rest of his clothing and stockings. Then he stood in all his naked glory.

Callie gasped, gripping the sheets beneath her and staring at him in wonder. His body was lean but corded with such beautiful muscles. That part of him that jutted proudly to her appeared flushed and thick. Yet instead of being afraid, her body jolted, and her legs fell apart with no urgings from him. He moved closer to the bed, staring down at her naked form. She blushed and fought the urge to drag the sheet over her.

She very much liked the awe and need on his face.

"You are beautifully made," he said in a low, smooth voice.

The bed dipped as he came over her. Her heart fluttered, and her body tensed and heated. As if with a mere touch, she would disintegrate. He kissed the tip of her nose, then her eyes, and finally her mouth with savage intensity for breath-taking moments.

He released her mouth to press a kiss to her forehead. Her lips burned in the aftermath of his fiery possession. Her lover's kisses lingered all over her blushing body. Her breasts surged at the intimacy of his caressing touch, and she moaned when his mouth closed over her nipple. It was as if lightning struck her low in her belly.

The sensations were hot and overwhelming. His hand seared a path over her quivering stomach down to her thighs. Then he was there, right where she ached the most. He rubbed her, and she almost fainted. She gripped his shoulders, her nails pressing deep into the muscles there as she held on for dear life. His fingers began a lust-arousing exploration of her soft, wet flesh. Callie gasped, and she trembled at that diabolical caress.

She had never imagined nothing this wonderful existed. A long finger slipped deep inside her feminine channel. A soft moan turned into a sob of raw need. It never occurred to restrain her responses or pretend demureness. Everything was too much for any form of modest indifference to his wicked lovemaking to rear its head.

She lay panting, chest heaving, desperate to process all the pleasures wreaking havoc through her body. He shifted slightly, bracing himself on one elbow so he could look at where he buried his index in her sex. Then he slipped another finger into the tightness of her body.

"Open for me, my sweet," he murmured with a mellow baritone.

She fisted the sheets and parted her legs more. His grunt of satisfaction said that was exactly what he needed. And somehow, his fingers burrowed even deeper, for she now felt a pinch of pain mingling with the awful pleasure.

*Oh!* It felt so naughty that he watched as he worked his digits inside her sex, witnessed the shaking of her thighs, and those instinctive rises of her hips. Irresistibly her gaze fell below his bent head...watching too as his fingers thrust and withdrew, building a fever of need right where he touched.

Another little sob came from her throat, and she gripped the sheets tighter.

"Graham," she gasped as his thumb glided over her nub of pleasure. The friction had her arching her hips more into his questing caress.

"Ah...that is it," he praised. "How wet you are getting for me, my Callisto."

She blushed at the sensual praise and the wanton way her legs had parted even wider.

"I am about to do something...alarming," he murmured, lifting his head to meet her stare. "I am not a small man, and I need to join with you here."

Apprehension reared its head as the memory of the thick stalk which had jutted from him. She wetted her lips. It had been far thicker than his fingers.

"How alarming?" she husked.

"I am going to kiss you...here," he said, rubbing along her nubbin and folds. "You'll get so wet for me, my sweet, so wet." He closed his eyes on a harsh groan, and she surmised that her wetness was an agreeable thing.

"Yes," she cried, needing the pleasure he promised.

He shifted lower and settled between her splayed thighs. The quick, heated lick across her folds ripped a wild cry from Callie as she processed the shock of terrible pleasure. He repeated his wicked, wicked caress. Her upper body came off the bed, only to have his hand flatten against her stomach, pressing her back as his lips covered her wet sex. He performed his devilish kiss several times until her body tensed, drawn tight as the pleasure built inside her until it broke, heat cascading through her.

Yet he did not stop. Tremors of ecstasy coursed

through her body, and she bit into her lip to stop the cries wanting to erupt from her. He licked her deep, and Callie cried out and gripped his hair with strength. Everything seemed as if it was spiraling out of control. His tongue flicked, and then his teeth scraped against her nub of pleasure. He rose above her, spreading her thighs in one powerful motion. A blunt but promising pressure notched at her slick entrance.

"You're so beautiful and responsive," he murmured, his blue eyes glittering with emotions she could not decipher.

"I can't help it," she whispered in a half groan, needing him to fill her.

With a powerful surge, he entered her, and Callie cried out, gripping his shoulders. The pain was shocking, and she stiffened beneath him. A sob escaped her, and he pressed a soothing kiss atop her forehead.

"It will soon pass," he promised, pressing a quick heated kiss on her mouth, distracting her from the awful pressure which had invaded her channel. She wanted to get his promise to never move, but soon her frantic thoughts were buried under the delight of his kisses.

Their mouths separated, and holding her gaze, her lover glided back and drove forward repeatedly, at times shallow, and then wonderfully hard and deep. Pleasure mingled with erotic pain, and she clasped his shoulders and hugged him to her as he did what he promised. He rode her, and it was such a wicked ride filling her with such wildness and bliss. Acting on the wanton urge beating in her blood, she wrapped her legs high around his hips. His groan of approval filled her with pleasure, and despite this shift pushing him even deeper inside her body and making the pressure in her sex more overwhelming, she climaxed with soul-searing intensity. He kissed her and seconds later, he hugged her into a tight embrace, and with a groan, found his own release.

# CHAPTER 10

The sun was lowering by the time Callie and Graham left the cottage. It felt like they had been there for days but according to his pocket watch, they had been missing for four hours.

Was that how long it took to fall hopelessly in love?

She stared at his patrician profile as he rowed them with powerful arm movements toward the shore. After her ravishment, she had lain in his arms, stunned at the enormity of what they had done. She had never understood how anyone could be carried away by passion and lead themselves to ruin, and now she realized how silly she had been before in her judgment.

From a kiss, he had consumed her, and she had willingly given him everything without reservation. Despite that, there was an anxious heaviness in her heart. He'd not said anything tender or anything that hinted he might want to court her. And it frightened her. Not because she had given him her virtue, but because he withdrew, and the possibility of happiness which she had seen as they laughed and talked over wine would vanish.

As if he sensed her stare, his regard shifted from the sky to her.

"The clouds are swollen," he jested, "is your nose twitching by any chance."

"No," she said softly.

His mouth curved in a tender smile. "Ah, then there is the hope we might make it back before more rain comes."

She nodded. Something wild and irrepressible in her had almost wished the rain had continued falling, forcing them to spend the night and not just a few hours together. They had talked some more in each other's arms and shared more kisses, which almost took a passionate turn. But when he had slipped a caressing finger between her legs, she had gasped and tightly closed them, shutting out his questing touch.

*Ah, you are sore.*

She still blushed to recall that statement, but he had been correct. He'd kissed her forehead and murmured an apology for being an insensitive lustful beast. She had snuggled into his arms as they had laughed and gossiped about the guests under his father's roof. As soon as the rain had eased, he had urged them from the bed, assisted her in dressing, and they tidied the cottage as best as they could.

Then they had struck out. She worried her bottom lip as the boat drew closer to the bank and the main house. Callie detected no one on the lawns.

"Do you think our absence was noted?"

"Perhaps not. Everyone would have to be together for it to be noticeable. Some guests would have been playing billiards or cards. Others would be in the drawing-room playing parlor games, some outside in the gazebo. Only at dinner when all the guests gather could anyone say decisively that we are missing. And we have another hour before the dinner gong. There will be enough time to make ourselves presentable and fashion credible excuses should anyone query."

"Do you...do you have trysts like these often?" a mortified flush ran along her entire body, but she would not take back her question.

His arms slowed, and the boat bobbed atop the waters of the lake. "We did not have a tryst," he replied slowly, his gaze scanning every nuance of her face.

"Then what did we have?" she asked her voice a broken whisper, gripping her fingers together. Callie couldn't understand what it was she needed from him, but her stomach knotted with dread. Everything inside of her ached.

"I do not know, but I have never had a lover where my entire body and heart was attuned to her," he husked. "I fear it might ruin me for all others."

"I shall celebrate it," she replied, meeting his intense regard.

Their stares held as he reached the dock, and in silence, he angled the craft in before hopping out to anchor it with the rope. Then he held his hand out. Callie grasped his arm and allowed him to assist her from the boat.

They had agreed earlier to enter through the kitchens and make use of the servants' stairwell. Callie entered first, and was clucked over by the cook, but made her way to her room encountering none of the houseguests, a thing she was most profoundly thankful for. Letty was sitting by the dressing table, the maid assigned to them styling her hair. Her sister's gaze searched her face, and whatever she saw prompted her to dismiss the maid.

"You were gone with the viscount for hours!"

"Oh, Letty! The rain kept us—"

"I gathered what we wanted happening to Mama occurred with you. Was he furious?"

"No," she said, her throat going tight. Callie normally shared everything with her sister, but this was too raw and private.

Letty stared at her. "I lied to Mama when she questioned your whereabouts about an hour ago. I told her I saw you in the private parlor reading. She seemed satisfied with that."

"Thank you, I daresay she would not care for us being forced to take shelter together."

"Are you well, Callie? You seem out of sorts," said Letty, with a quizzical look at her sister.

"Yes, most certainly!" She hurried over to the screen and started to remove her clothing.

Letty came over and took Callie's hands between hers. "Your lips are swollen, and I can tell they have been kissed *thoroughly*."

Heat flushed Callie's neck and face. "Oh!"

Her sister grinned. "Is he an excellent kisser?"

"The most wonderful, oh Letty, *everything* was so divine!" Then she shocked herself by sobbing. "My blasted nerves are overset when they should not be!"

"You do not have to tell me now," Letty said with a warm smile, "because dinner will be announced soon. I'll ring for a bath and select a dress for you!"

Grateful to her sister, she nodded, and proceeded to undress, not understanding the bewildering mix of hope and anxiety in her heart.

DINNER HAD BEEN a sumptuous feast of roasted duck with cranberry sauce, standing ribs of beef with Yorkshire pudding, golden stuffed turkey, lamb served with an onion sauce. She had tried her best not to stare at Graham throughout the meal, and the few times she had done so had been to find the man staring at her. He had mastered himself and behaved gentlemanly for the rest of the evening, only engaging her in polite dinner conversation. But he had given other ladies equal attention.

Almost three hours later, the earl had gathered his

guests in the drawing-room. An enormous spruce tree had been cut and placed in the corner near the windows overlooking the lawns. They had decorated the tree with enormous bows of bright scarlet ribbon, precious glass baubles, and silver candle holders with white candles.

The earl cleared his throat, and the young lady who had been playing a lively piece on the pianoforte stopped. The drawing-room door opened, and she glanced over her shoulder to see that Graham had entered drinking a glass of amber liquid. She stared at him for longer than what was polite, and when he noted her regard, he winked. Swallowing her gasp of pleasure, she turned back to the earl who seemed as if he was fit to burst at the seams.

Callie's heart jolted when he held out his hand, and her mother walked forward with a bright, gleeful smile on her face to place her hand within his. Letty sent her a side-eye glance.

"It is with pleasure I announce to you all that Lady Danby has consented to be my wife, and we are to wed tomorrow in the chapel."

There was a stunned silence before everyone burst into applause. Congratulations went around, and the earl shepherded Callie, Letty, Graham, and his daughter to the smaller private parlor. As they entered, Callie spun to face them. "The wedding is tomorrow?"

"Yes," her mother said, smiling. How happy she looked.

"So soon mamma?" Callie asked, stunned at this development.

""Robert says he will not give me a chance to change my mind. But I shall not. He has summoned the vicar from the town village, and the servants will decorate the chapel with hothouse flowers, evergreens, holly, and lots of mistletoe! Girls, I am so happy! And Callie, I know how you've always longed for an older brother to indulge your eccentricities."

A sinking sensation entered her belly. "Brother?" she parroted. "What brother?"

"Yes," a voice proffered from behind, then Graham came into view. "Earlier, my father informed me of the joyful news and reminded me how thrilled I should be in getting two new sisters. I am delighted, of course."

There was a dark, sarcastic edge to his tone she found discomfiting. *Brother and sister?*

A sick sense of unreality crept through Callie. With trembling fingers, she pushed a strand of hair behind her ear. In a daze, she glanced at Letty, who was staring at her with concern.

*Is all well?* Her sister mouthed.

Her throat burning, Callie attempted to smile. It wobbled, then emerged, but it felt like a baring of her teeth. She nodded, hating the slow, painful, and unfamiliar emotions twisting through her.

"My boy!" the earl said with boisterous joviality. "Come closer."

He stepped forward, and father and son hugged fiercely. "I am happy for you, Father," he said gruffly.

Then he released the earl and turned to her mother and gave her the most charming yet respectful bow. "Welcome to our family, Lady Danby."

Her mother laughed, delight glowing in her eyes. "Oh please, do not be so formal!" she hugged him and upon releasing him, lifted her gaze to his and said, "I would not object should you wish to call me Mo...Mother."

He flinched, his expression shifting from open warmth to an unfathomable visage.

"Not now I mean," her mother said in a horrified tone. "Or not ever...only if you are comfortable, or you could just call me..."

Her husband rested a hand on her shoulder. "My dear, my son knows what you mean," he said with a tender smile.

The viscountess released a sigh, and some tension left her shoulders. "I fear I am a bit nervous. This was all so wonderful but unexpected." She sent a careful glance at Callie. "I sensed some undercurrents between you earlier by the lake, and I gather you dislike the viscount. I am asking you to make a credible effort in getting to know him since he will be your older brother. Robert assures me his son's forbidding and arrogant countenance hides a warm heart, and I do so much want our family to be happy!"

It was Callie's turn to flinch, and she wrapped her hands around her middle, the memory of his body penetrating hers...the pain and then that excruciating pleasure. The knowledge that she could love him... that she wanted him to overwhelm her senses.

"My dear," her mother said with a worried frown. "Are you well? You seem rather flushed."

"I...we...we were caught in the rain."

"How selfish of me! The rain started only a few minutes after your outing."

"No, Mama," Callie said, gripping her hands. "You are not selfish at all. I am so delighted for you."

Her mother hugged her and whispered, "Thank you for all your naughty mischief. We needed that nudge."

Over her mother's shoulder, she spied Graham, watching them with an unfathomable expression in his gaze. Then without another word, he turned and left the room. Callie reflected that with his departure, he took all the earlier hope she had felt and left behind the awful disquiet.

GRAHAM RODE along the lanes of Holliwell Manor, inhaling the cold crisp air into his lungs. He'd had a most restless night, and hoped an invigorating run would clear his thoughts. It was damned difficult to do when he felt like he did not understand the past day. His father was getting married to the viscountess. He was happy for his father and Graham

STACY REID

saw that the attachment between the pair was genuine. The manner in which the viscountess stared at his father had been quite revealing and it had laid the doubts in his heart to rest.

The sound of hooves thundered close, and he shifted in his saddle to watch the approach of his father. Graham waited until he stopped beside him before urging his horse into a trot. His father kept his slow, steady pace until they entered deeper into the park woodlands.

"In a few hours I will be married," his father began gruffly.

"I know," Graham said quietly. "I am truly happy for you father."

He cleared his throat before turning his horse so that he faced his son directly.

Graham arched a brow. "What is it?"

"Whatever you are thinking in relation to Callisto cannot happen."

It felt like a shard of ice pierced his gut. "You do not know my thoughts in regard to her father."

"I saw enough of the need in your face when you stared at her last night!" His father's face grew thunderous. "I saw lust! For your sister. It is unseemly that you would look at Callie in such a lustful manner. I observed you last night, and you will treat her as your sister at all times."

Graham's hand tightened on the reins and anger scythed through his heart. "She is not my damn sister! And I am certain you saw more than desire, father, because I feel much more for her than mere lust."

His father stiffened. "By God, you've already ruined her."

Graham felt the tip of his ears heating and scowled. "She...she is not ruined."

"The hours in the cabin," his father said through gritted teeth. "Whatever happened will never occur again. I will have your word as my son and a gentleman."

He stared at his father, a heavy boulder settling against his chest. "And if I cannot give you my word to stay away from her?"

"Then I will cancel the wedding with Viscountess Danby, and you can go and pursue her daughter."

Graham scrubbed a hand over his face. "Father, this is ridiculous—"

"The scandal of the father marrying the wife and the son dallying with his stepsister is not something to dismiss lightly," his father said, his eyes hard and unforgiving. "Do you love her?"

The words slammed into Graham and robbed him of speech. Did he love her? He had no idea if this all-consuming desire he possessed for Callie was love. Was this love? This burning need to cherish, protect, and make love her always. "Father, I—"

"That is what I thought," his father said tightly. "You will claim her as your sister and nothing else. If that is a problem for you my son, you will keep your distance until you have learned to govern your damn self!"

Anger snapped through his veins, for he had been certain in the long and lonely night in his room, that he wanted her with every breath in his body. He was falling for her...possibly in love with her.

"By God, she is not my sister," he said with raw intensity. "And I will never see her in such a manner, and it is ridiculous to expect it of me."

"What are you saying?" his father demanded, fisting his hands at his side.

"I want her..." Graham whispered. "Father...I want her more than anything I've ever wanted in my life."

His father's eyes darkened with pain and ire. "Well, you cannot have her. It is wrong that you would even think it. I am to marry her mother in a few hours. You will become siblings through marriage. Can you imagine the scandal such a thing would cause? Everyone would repudiate such connections. The father marrying the mother and the son marrying the daughter of the mother. It will be seen as incestuous!"

"Do not be a damn fool!" Graham snapped, even though he detected a kernel of truth in his father's assessment. "Since when did you give a damn about what Society thinks?"

"There are many other women you can take as your mistress—"

"I do not mean to use her," Graham replied,

raking his fingers through his hair. "Do you think so low of my character, that I would dishonor her in such a crude manner? I want to court her...eventually, marry her."

His father was silent for a long time, then he said, "I will never consent to it."

"I do not need your approval."

Anger flushed along his father's cheekbones. "You've only been aware of her for several damnable days. You cannot be certain of your feelings, and I am certain whatever they are, they will fade. There will be no scandal, nor will I cause Amelia any discomfort! And I am also fairly certain Miss Callie is indifferent to you! By God, I am happy...Amelia is happy, a state neither of us has been in years. I will not have you marring that joy for either of us with scandal or speculation! I'll have her mother ship that girl away if that is what it will take."

Then he turned around and rode away in self-righteous fury, leaving Graham feeling hollowed and empty.

CHAPTER 11

The Holliwell Manor Chapel had been constructed by an earlier ancestor during King Charles II's reign. Built on the edge of the estate, it had served the village until they had built a new and larger church in the last century. Now its use was scant; although the local vicar held an occasional service there during the year. Most of those services were to commemorate former members of the Wynter family who had gone to their eternal rest.

It was a small stone building with narrow windows, and despite the staff's best efforts to warm the interior, it was still chilly when the house party guests drove down to the chapel to observe the nuptials of Robert Wynter, Earl of Deerwood who would marry Amelia Middleton, Viscountess of Danby. The Manor's staff had been busy decorating the interior with greenery and hothouse flowers while trying to drive out the seeping cold within the old building. The chapel already was half full as the news of the earl's sudden wedding had spread through the local village, so most of his tenants and neighbors with their families had appeared uninvited to share in their lord's joy.

Yet he was not joyful. For conflicting emotions tore through Graham.

The memory of the fight he had with his father a couple hours ago had his heart icing over.

*Do I love you, Callie?*

Her laugh made him happy, just seeing her filled his heart with joy. And the memory of the way she had taken him into her body had him biting back a groan. She was the most incredible lover he'd ever had, but it was more than that. Graham wanted to fulfill every need and hunger he had spied in her eyes as they had talked in the cabin. He wanted to lay all her dreams at her feet and provide his shoulders to rest upon whenever she needed them.

He had never been a man given to flights of fancy or over-sentimentality, and that was how he had known the feelings rushing through his heart and tormenting his mind were the deepest of *tendre*.

Graham glanced at his father. He was already waiting by the altar, walking up and down agitated and trying not to fiddle with the neat arrangement of his cravat. The earl had worn a golden silk waistcoat with a pale gray suit of clothes for his special day. He looked dashing despite his impatience for his bride to arrive.

Despite their argument, Graham had agreed to be his best man, so he waited with him, somewhat amused by his father's nerves. They had greeted the tenants and neighbors who had appeared at the church and shaken many hands. The chapel was far enough from the house in this inclement weather to necessitate them driving along the lanes in a stream of carriages, which had deposited them at the chapel door before parking as best they could. For the coachmen, it would be a cold wait.

Among the guests, there were undercurrents of excitement, surprise, and some chagrin by Miss Penelope Barrows over the unexpected marriage of so sought-after a groom. They were still gossiping together as they filed into the chapel to find their seats. As the last guest seated, a hush settled over the small gathering as they waited for the bride. They were listening for one last carriage to appear, and then in the distance, they heard the clip-clop of the earl's high-stepping matched grays, as he had decided his best team should honor the bride on their wedding day.

The carriage pulled up outside the old ivy-clad chapel, and a footman raced to let the step down. The three bridesmaids gracefully descended, all dressed in white, although their dresses did not match; they had chosen to be warmly wrapped in festive shawls of scarlet, crimson, and green. His sister, Emma, who would become their stepsister had joined Callie and Letty.

*Christ*. As he would become their stepbrother.

Graham did his best not to stare at Callie's loveliness. This morning she wore a low-cut white gown, with her hair caught in a loose chignon. She met his eyes, and her cheeks blushed apple red. Then she hurriedly looked away. He tore his gaze from her and concentrated on the carriage, hating the heaviness forming in his heart.

They waited while the bride was handed out. Lady Danby wore a pale blue gown she had covered with her dark gray cloak to travel the scant distance to the chapel. She shrugged off its warmth to enter the church, and Callie handed it to the footman. Sometime overnight they had located a long cream veil in priceless Chantilly lace upon which was set a small diamond tiara, which was part of the Wynter family jewels. Bouquets of ivy and white roses had been made, and each of the girls carried a smaller version of the one the viscountess carried herself. The bride had chosen not to be given away as she was a widow, an orphan, and of age. So she would walk down the short aisle alone, followed by her daughters and soon to be stepdaughter.

The chapel was not provided with an organ or piano to accompany the congregation, but a string quartet who had been employed for the house party entertainment had been installed in the choir stalls and struck up a pretty piece of music by Purcell for Lady Danby to process to.

Evidently trying to ease her nerves, she waited

until the first phrases had floated through the chapel, and then she plant a joyful smile on her face. As the sweet music floated through her, she relaxed, and the smile became genuine. She straightened her back and set a dignified slow march down the aisle, followed by the three lovely girls in white. When she reached the front of the chapel, she handed her bouquet to Callie and smiled at her groom. The bridesmaids took the seats reserved for them and waited while their parents were led in their vows.

Throughout the ceremony, Graham only had eyes for Callie, and she did her best to not look in his direction. Was she genuinely indifferent to him, and yesterday in the cottage had simply been a once only experience for her?

The idea that she might feel nothing for him gnawed at his gut. The rest of the ceremony and wedding breakfast passed in a blur.

"I've always wanted a Christmas wedding," he heard the new countess say at one point. "But I thought that delight would be reserved for one of my daughters."

"Oh Mama," Callie said, laughing. "I am glad it was you! I am certain I will remain a spinster."

"Oh, pish! That lovely Dr. Harcourt couldn't stop staring at you today. I daresay he will come calling soon."

As if caressed by his stare, Callie glanced up at him. She didn't reject her mother's claim; she only stared back at him. When the countess saw him, she beamed. "Here comes your new brother!"

Sweet Christ, it was torturous. He wanted to roar he was not her bloody brother but gravely kept his lips sealed. The cravat seemed to tighten around his throat when a mocking smile tipped Callisto's lips, and she greeted,

"Hello, Brother."

Ice filled his veins as he glanced at her with utter disbelief. "Ah...sister Callisto," he quipped.

Graham wasn't sure what she saw in his face, but the sarcastic smile slipped from her mouth, and she laced her fingers together.

"We must make the best of the situation," she said with quiet emphasis, casting a careful glance at her mother, to ensure the countess did not overhear. But she was busy receiving congratulations from her guests. "Our parents are very happy."

"And what does their happiness have to do with us?"

She peered up at him and he could see the wild fluttering of her pulse at her throat. "Will there be an us?"

Instead of paying attention to his new bride, his father was busy staring at them and looking worried. His countess frowned and leaned in close to whisper in his ears. That still did not detract the earl's attention from his son and new daughter.

Callie seemed to notice and flushed in evident

discomfort. "Your father...he cannot stop watching us."

And in that moment Graham knew he could not stay for the rest of the house party. He sketched a deep bow to Callisto. "I suppose we must make the best of the situation. I am leaving Holliwell Manor today."

Her eyes widened, and she reached out and gripped his gloved hand. "What...why?"

When she realized what she had done, she released him as if seared by fire.

"My father has warned me away from you. In fact, he is truly angry at the idea that we might like each other."

"He is afraid of what society might whisper," she said, closing her eyes briefly.

His heart was a pained ache inside his chest. "I need your promise on a matter."

Tears pooled in her gaze, but they did not spill over. "What is it?"

"If there are any consequences to yesterday...you will inform me immediately."

Her lips parted and fear, stark and vivid, glittered in her eyes. "Consequences," she whispered. "Do you mean a...a child?"

His gaze dipped to her stomach and lingered there for an inordinate amount of time. "Yes," he grumbled. He had lost his head and hadn't thought about protecting her until after they had finished making love. "A child."

She rested a hand protectively across her middle. "And if there are?"

"Then we will marry and damn the scandal."

Pain darkened her eyes, and she stared at him. "I...I see."

When she said no more, he sketched another bow and walked away, confident she should reach out to him if needed. He wished his father and new mother well, before calling for his horse and made his way from the swell of happiness behind him.

Graham rode away, hating the piercing pain that flamed through him. How it had all shot to hell so quickly, his muddled brain still had to figure out. *It is for the best*, he tried to tell himself. Except he felt as if he were riding away from the best thing that ever happened to him, instead of hurtling toward Callisto with his heart and arms wide open.

# CHAPTER 12

*Christmas day*

It was mid-afternoon, and the day was filled with laughter, and a sense of hope and expectation blanketed the air. Over the night, there had been snow, and a pristine white blanketed the grass and dotted the trees and shrubs of the estate. It was such a beautiful scene that Callie's heart was saddened she could not share it with Graham. It had been all she could do to attend the Parish Church the night before for midnight mass with her family, she had gone through the motions although it had taken every bit of determination she had. Now where she stood on the path beside the lake, Callie fancied she could smell the sumptuous feast the servants were busy and joyfully preparing in the kitchens, although she was not looking forward to another meal pretending to be happy so she did not wear her heart on her sleeve.

A flake caressed her cheek, she glanced to the sky which had darkened even further, the chill in the air had her hugging her coat closer. Despite the festivities Callie was bereft of joy. Graham had departed Holliwell Manor over a week ago now, and to Callie's enduring distress each night, she cried herself to sleep. She hadn't realized the consequences attached to her reckless bid to taste passion, and worse the viscount seemed only willing to marry her if she was with child. The wintry weather reflected the desolation in her heart, everything around her mirrored the merry season but she was so miserable and alone.

Though she desired him with every breath in her body, she did not want him in that manner, where he would be forced to do the honorable thing for the sake of her reputation and their child. Once again, her breath hitched and a deep yearning scythed through her chest. A child...a husband...a family of her own.

How badly she wanted it all! But that other longing to marry a man whom she loved and one who adored her just as ardently would not be a part of that bargain. How cold and indifferent Graham had appeared, and she could only blame herself for being silly to have such expectations in her heart.

They did not know each other! Perhaps the passion they had shared had been an everyday occurrence for him. And he did not appreciate the laughter they had enjoyed, for he had just been toying with her affections to pass the time. Could it be the tender way he had looked at her was in her imagination or a cynical act to allow him to bed her. Maybe she had irrevocably lost all sense of herself when she gifted him her body. And she had imagined the hunger in his eyes when he had stared at her stomach as if picturing she was already with child.

But she was not. She swallowed. Her menses had arrived yesterday, and she had cried even more. For deep inside, she had been willing to marry him with their child, madly tying them together, and then she had vowed to make him fall in love with her. It wouldn't matter how or why they married, only that she would ensure their happiness.

Only now...she had no reason to write to him, and he had none to visit her.

She raised trembling fingers to her lips, hating that her throat burned with tears. Callie didn't think she would ever recover from the storm of the last few days over the years to come. He had captured her heart, and when he had left, he took it with him.

"I want it back," she cried in a sharp sob. "If I do not have yours, you cannot have mine!" *I'll storm his estate and demand it back*, she fumed. Yes, that is what she would do. Travel to his estate before he could return to town and demand a straightforward explanation of his affections for her. It could not be that the day in the cottage had been meaningless, she refused to accept that it was all lies. With that new resolve in her heart, she felt a little lighter even if the painful ache still lingered.

"Callie?"

She whirled around to see her mother approaching her, looking radiant and contented.

"Mama," she said with a wobbly smile. "Happy Christmas to you."

"The same to you, my dear," she said with a bright smile.

Her eyes searched Callie's face. "Callie, I cannot help but notice how morose you've been. I fretted over it, but then Robert confided in me just now of what the potential problem might be."

Callie frowned, she had believed that she had hidden her feelings so well. What did the earl know of her heartache? "Mama—"

"He told me of Graham asking to court you, and of the argument which followed. Is it that you were also open to your bro...to the viscount's courtship?"

She hesitated, blinking her bafflement. "Graham asked to court me?"

*He is truly angry at the idea that we might like each other.*

"Yes...and it seemed my dear Robert objected strongly, and they quarreled most fiercely."

Callie's vision swam, and she took a deep breath to right herself. "It is ridiculous he would object," she said crossly.

"The scandal would be lurid—"

"The earl expects us to rest our happiness on the possibilities that people in Society might not approve," Callie snapped in angry astonishment. "Mama! I like him so very much...I am falling hopelessly in love with him, I am certain of it. We are not brothers and sisters. It is simply outrageous to ask us to act against our heart desires. What about *our* happiness? What about my happiness, mama?"

"My dear you speak nonsense—"

"No...I am not." Callie kissed her mama's cheek and hurried away, then broke into a run.

She skidded on the snow-soaked grass when she saw a rumpled Graham heading toward her. He appeared as if he had ridden hard to reach Holliwell Manor, and he had a shadow of a beard.

How utterly rakish and wonderful he looked!

He stood before her, and his presence filled all the emptiness she had endured for the past week with such hope, she trembled. They stared at each other, his gaze skimming her features.

Callie could only stare, tongue-tied. Finally, she said, "Graham? Why...why are you here?"

"I was a fool."

A harsh breath left her, but she made no reply.

"I have never wanted anyone or anything in the way I do you. But it is more than a physical want, Callie, I feel it here," he said pressing a hand over his heart. "Most keenly. Most desperately."

Her lips trembled and her eyes burned. "I am not with child."

"I am not here because I hope you are with child." He reached for her, tugged her tight into his arms, and with a groan, he slanted his mouth over hers as if the tether on his control had snapped. The kiss was one of violent tenderness, and it communicated such longing and regret, tears burned behind her eyes. Their mouths parted, and his thumb swiped tenderly over her lips.

"It has only been eight days, but I missed you so damn much!" Then he placed another kiss at the corner of her mouth.

"You left me," she said against his mouth with a sob. "With such uncertainty and pain, a living entity in my heart."

"I am so sorry," he whispered.

"I am not likely to forgive you!"

But then she hugged him to her in a fierce embrace.

He stepped away from her and cupped her chin. "Forgive my momentarily lapse from common sense," he said gruffly. "I rode home to Hampshire, resting my horse each night while I slept at inns. Once home, I knew I had to come back right away. I was a damn fool for leaving without expressing to you the hopes I had toward you. I am falling so deeply in love with you…I just might be there already."

Her entire body flushed at the raw hunger, which leaped into his eyes.

My heart…my entire being feels enmeshed with

yours. Callisto...will you allow me to court you...to marry you?"

Her mother gasped, and Callie glanced over her shoulder to see Mama's eyes growing wide with astonishment and shock. Turning back to Graham, she released a breath she hadn't known she held then she hugged him again.

"What about the earl, he is adamantly opposed to the idea of us being together?"

"Do you need his approval?"

"No, but I do not want us to hurt the people who we love."

"We won't, but nothing will ever force me away from you. No scandal and certainly not my father's disapproval. He grew me to know my own mind and heart and I will most certainly remind him of that."

"Be certain, for I shall not allow you to break your promises!"

He touched the corner of her mouth tenderly. "I'll not break them. Trust me with your heart, your friendship, and your love, please."

"Yes!" Callie cried. "I'll allow you to woo me, Graham."

"And marry you?"

"Maybe," she said in a low, sensual voice. "Who knows if I'll like your courtship?"

With a soft chuckle, he said, "Challenge accepted."

Then he held out his arms, and they strolled together toward the main house.

# EPILOGUE

*London St James's Church, Hanover Square*

It was to be the wedding of the Season, and everyone who was anyone in the *ton* had been invited. The church was packed to the rafters, and everyone was agog to see what the bride would wear. Miss Callisto Middleton had been the acknowledged diamond of the Season, despite being older than the debutantes who had expected that plaudit to have been awarded them.

Callie had found the experience very strange. Since her mother, the Countess of Deerwood, had launched her anew into Society, and despite the obvious way Viscount Sherbrooke courted her in earnest, she had many suitors who were apparently enamored of her delicate charms. However, Callie suspected few would have shown so much determination to woo her without the dowry of ten thousand pounds her step-father had settled on her.

Callie and Letty had lapped up the attention, the flowers, the balls where neither of them had the chance to sit out a single dance and all the other excitement from their stay in Town at the earl's magnificent townhouse.

But in her heart, there had only been Graham. Since that one time they had made love in the cottage, he hadn't attempted to seduce her again. It had been a lesson in restraint. One night as they had scandalously danced every dance together at a midnight ball he had whispered, "I am dying to taste you and love you again...but upon my honor I will wait until our wedding night."

That had been over four months ago.

The gossips of the *ton* took pleasure in discussing the courtship of Miss Middleton and Viscount Sherbrooke. Some commented with shock and distaste, while others did so with open admiration and gentle encouragement of their union. Each day she had fallen in love with him on a deeper level, and Callie felt such happiness that today she would finally be his wife. Earlier the townhouse had been pandemonium as servants rushed to make sure everything was perfect for the wedding breakfast of Lady Callisto Sherbrooke and her beloved Graham, Viscount Sherbrooke.

Closing her eyes and taking a deep breath, she entered the church. All the whispers died down, and an air of anticipation throbbed through all the family and guests. Graham waited for her, resplendent in navy-blue trousers and matching jacket, an expertly tied cravat, and a green silken waistcoat. The look of awe and love on his face pierced Callie with the sweetest feelings. They had caught her hair in the most elegant of chignons with becoming wisps framing her face, and a coronet of flowers woven between the strands. She wore the most beautiful high-waisted ivory silk gown seeded with pearls.

*You are beautiful*, he mouthed, the love in his eyes on display for the world to see. *I love you.*

With a trembling laugh, she walked towards him, never taking her eyes from his. *I love you so*, she mouthed. She reached his side, and he reached out and took her gloved hand between his. Her whole being filled with wonder and reflected in his eyes she saw the same emotions whispering through his heart.

The earl grunted that he was giving her away before taking his seat.

The bishop began the ceremony. "Dearly beloved, we are gathered together here in the sight of God, and in the face of this congregation, to join together this man and this woman in holy matrimony, which is an honorable estate..."

Callie could not prevent the wide smile that curved her lips when Graham winked. She had to restrain the urge to fling herself in his arms and hug him.

The bishop turned to him, "Graham George

Winter, Viscount Sherbrooke, wilt thou have this woman to thy wedded wife, to live together after God's ordinance in the holy estate of matrimony? Wilt thou love her, comfort her, honor, and keep her in sickness and in health; and, forsaking all other, keep thee only unto her, so long as ye both shall live?"

"I will," he vowed, the curve of a smile tipping his mouth.

The bishop shifted to Callie.

"Miss Callisto Georgiana Middleton, wilt thou have this man to thy wedded husband, to live together after God's ordinance in the holy estate of matrimony? Wilt thou obey him, and serve him, love, honor, and keep him in sickness and in health; and, forsaking all other, keep thee only unto him, so long as ye both shall live?"

"I will," she said with a voice that trembled, then she smiled.

A few seconds later, they were declared man and wife. Callie laughed, the sound light and joyous. And as if he could not help himself, Graham drew her to him and pressed a kiss to her forehead, then over her nose, and then softly on her lips, ignoring the tittering of the guests in the pews. Powerful emotions darkened his eyes. "I love you, Callisto, most ardently."

"And I love you," she uttered her voice fragile and shaky.

"Now, let's go home," he murmured. "Then we'll honeymoon in Italy and Paris."

*Home.* Lacing their gloved hands together, they turned down the aisle and walked toward their future, which promised happiness.

*Several hours later...*

THE LARGE WELL-PADDED and heated equipage they had been travelling in for a few hours rumbled to a stop. The steps were knocked down, and Graham assisted Callie from the carriage.

"This is our home?" She asked with a gasp of wonder.

An avenue of beech trees lined the long driveway leading to a magnificent manor with a sweeping arched entrance. The estate grounds were glorious and there was a large lake abutting the property. She could see a few boats bobbing on the water. "I am to be mistress here?"

Graham wrapped his hands around her waist and pressed a kiss at the corner of her neck. "Yes. This is the manor I spent the last few months restoring. I suspected you would fall in love with its charm."

"Our home is so very beautiful, Graham," she whispered. Callie had known he had been working hard on restoring a manor that sat just on the outskirts of London town.

"It was originally constructed in the Tudor times." He turned her and press a kiss to her mouth.

"You are going to scandalize the servants," she

said with a laugh, noting the line of servants at the forecourt.

"Let them be shocked. Best they get used to me kissing you. I thought we could spend this year here. Unless you wish to travel to town for the season after our honeymoon is over."

"No, this is perfect, my love, thank you." Callie hadn't wanted to stay in town much, especially with the few lingering gossips that surrounded their family. She did not want to give those busy bodies her energy, but to direct all her efforts on keeping her family safe and contented.

"This is just one of our country homes, but I was hoping we could make it our main residence. We could spend a week or two here, and then escape to Paris for the first part of our honeymoon and then onto Italy."

She turned in the cage of his arms. "My home is where you are."

"We also do not have a name for our newest manor. The previous owner called it Williamsfield Hall in honor of his grandfather. Would you do the honor?"

She grinned, delighted. "It would be my pleasure."

Soon she was introduced to the line of smartly dressed servants and then was led inside for a tour of the palatial property. More than an hour later, she swallowed her giggles several times at the fierce scowls Graham kept sending the housekeeper who jubilantly showed her room after room. The servants seemed incredibly pleased he was their master, and even happier that he had settled down.

"Mrs. Hays," Graham said, interrupting the housekeeper with a pained smile. "I fear we must cut the tour short today. My wife and I desperately need to confer."

She bobbed her head. "I'll have supper prepared in the blue dining—"

"We'll take trays in our room a few hours from now."

The housekeeper's eyes widened, and Callie blushed. Mrs. Hays dipped into a quick curtsey and then hurried away a smile on her mouth.

Before Callie could say anything, he swept her into his arms. "You rogue," she said laughing and leaning in to press a soft kiss to his jaw.

He hurried with her down the hallway to stop before a door. Her husband deftly opened the door without dropping her and carried her into the center of the room. The décor was a blur and she could not direct her thought on it when her husband tried to untie his cravat with trembling fingers. Callie smiled to see how much he wanted her.

She reached up onto her toes and smashed her lips to his, kissing him with all the love and happiness in her heart. He stilled, and a sigh slipped from his mouth to hers.

"How I've waited for this," he murmured. "I am in awe that you are now my wife."

"Is that why you pinched yourself a few times in the carriage," she teased.

"Notice that did you?"

He lovingly framed her cheeks with his hands and kissed her with gentle thoroughness. They slowly undressed each other, at times fumbling and laughing, and pausing to indulge in long, ravishing kisses.

Once they were naked, he lifted Callie and placed her in the center of the bed. Graham kissed along her cheek, down to her neck, and then the heated wetness of his tongue tormented the tender tips of her nipples until she moaned his name. Callie arched her back, her fingers gripping and twisting the silken sheets below her heated body. Her husband drove her to madness with his diabolical tongue.

His lips dragged against the soft of her belly, firm and velvety, stoking a feverish heat beneath her skin. Then he was there, kissing her sex until she arched her hips off the bed screaming his name. What he was doing...it *had* to be a sin, but such a glorious sin.

He licked her over and over again until her breaths became gasping cries. She hadn't known a pleasure like this existed. Her fingers clenched tighter on the sheets beneath her as he licked and nibbled with decadent greed. When his lips closed over her nub, suckling hard, she hurtled over the edge with a wild scream which echoed in the room. Her husband crawled over her and settled between her splayed legs. The look on his face was one of lust and sweet tenderness.

Callie's heart clenched and she traced a finger gently over his cheekbone. "How I love you," she breathed.

With a deep groan, he kissed her tenderly, barely brushing his lips over hers. "I am so glad you are mine, Callie. I *love* you."

He kissed the bridge of her nose and then down to her lips. The taste of her passion on his mouth enflamed her ardor even more. His mouth consumed her, possessed her, laying claim with each bold thrust of his tongue. She parted her lips for his tongue, moaning as he plundered her softness. He cupped her jaw firmly, sensually as he ravished her mouth.

With his other hand, he fitted his cock to her opening and sheathed himself in one thrust. Her wild cry was captured by his mouth, and he held himself still and allow her body to adjust to his thick, throbbing intrusion. He stopped kissing her to murmur against her mouth, "You grip me so hot and tight, my Callie."

The fingers stroking over her jaw lowered. His thumbs swiped over her nipples, before capturing the hard pebble between his thumbs and forefingers. He bent his head, drew one delicate berry into his mouth.

She gripped his shoulders, her fingers kneading the muscles of his shoulders, then slipped her hands around his neck. His throat was a strong, corded column beneath her feather-light touch.

"Graham!" she gasped at the raw heat blossoming

through her at a particular hard suck of her throbbing nipples.

She wrapped her arms around him and pulled him even closer. His tongue flicked over her aching nipple, laving it over and again. That wicked heat gathered inside of her once more, except this time it felt *more* than what had happened in the cabin at Holliwell Manor. When he started to move inside her, it was with exquisite depth and slowness.

A wonderfully intense sensation twisted low in her stomach. He stroked into her over and over, ignoring her wild cries urging him faster. What felt like hours later, Callie clung to her husband and let pleasure consumed her, a long, low moan breaking from her lips at the exquisite bliss. She sobbed with the ecstasy of her own surrender and with a deep groan he tumbled into bliss with her.

Graham rolled with her, so she was splayed atop his chest. He dipped and pressed a kiss to her temple. "I love you, Callie."

"I love you," she murmured with drowsy contentment, then fell asleep with a smile on her lips and pure, unguarded happiness in her heart.

***

*Thank you for reading* **Mischief and Mistletoe**, *novella ten in my Forever Yours series!* I hope you enjoyed the journey to happy ever after for Callie and Graham.

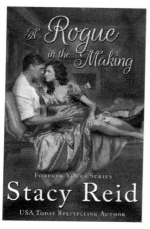

PRE-ORDER *A ROGUE IN THE MAKING*, the next sexy and fun book in the Forever Yours series! Featuring a very proper and scholarly earl not interested in love or passion, until he discovers an heiress hiding in his home under the guise of being his valet!

*Order it Now!*

REVIEWS ARE GOLD TO AUTHORS, for they are a very important part of reaching readers. I do hope you will consider leaving an honest review on Amazon adding to my rainbow. It does not have to be lengthy, a simple sentence or two will do. Just know that I will appreciate your efforts sincerely.

Thank you,
Stacy

## FREE OFFER
### SIGN UP TO MY NEWSLETTER TO CLAIM YOUR FREE BOOK!

To claim your FREE copy of Wicked Deeds on a Winter Night, a delightful and sensual romp to indulge in your reading addiction, please click here.

Once you've signed up, you'll_be among the first to hear about my new releases, read excerpts you won't find anywhere else, and patriciate in subscriber's only giveaways and contest. I send out on dits once a month and on super special occasion I might send twice, and please know you can unsubscribe whenever we no longer zing.

Happy reading!
Stacy Reid

## ACKNOWLEDGMENTS

I thank God every day for my family, friends, and writing. A special thank you to my husband. I love you so hard! You encourage me to dream and are always steadfast in your incredible support. You read all my drafts, offer such fantastic insight and encouragement. Thank you for designing my fabulous cover! Thank you for reminding me I am a warrior when I wanted to give up on so many things.

Thank you, Giselle Marks for being so wonderful and supportive always. You are a great critique partner and friend.

Readers, thank you for giving me a chance and reading my book! I hope you enjoyed and would consider leaving a review. Thank you!

# ABOUT STACY

Stacy Reid writes sensual Historical and Paranormal Romances and is the published author of over sixteen books. Her debut novella The Duke's Shotgun Wedding was a 2015 HOLT Award of Merit recipient in the Romance Novella category, and her bestselling Wedded by Scandal series is recommended as Top picks at Night Owl Reviews, Fresh Fiction Reviews, and The Romance Reviews.

Stacy lives a lot in the worlds she creates and actively speaks to her characters (aloud). She has a warrior way "Never give up on dreams!" When she's not writing, Stacy spends a copious amount of time binge-watching series like The Walking Dead, Homeland, Altered Carbon, watching Japanese Anime and playing video games with her love. She also has a weakness for ice cream and will have it as her main course.

I am always happy to hear from readers and would love to connect with you via my Website, Facebook, and Twitter. To be the first to hear about my new releases, get cover reveals, and excerpts you won't find anywhere else, sign up for my newsletter, or join me over at Historical Hellions, the fan group for my historical romance author friends, and me!

Printed by Amazon Italia Logistica S.r.l.
Torrazza Piemonte (TO), Italy

16716820R00084